# SECRETS IN SAVANNAH

## THE SOUTHERN SLEUTH BOOK 3

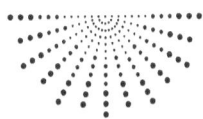

### HARPER LIN

ISBN: 978-1-987859-77-5

www.harperlin.com

# CHAPTER ONE

SAVANNAH, GEORGIA, 1922

illie's Club was jumping. The cool weather outside had driven everyone within a fifty-mile radius to this tucked-away speakeasy. The dance floor was packed like a can of sardines. Bathtub gin and champagne were flowing like the Savannah River. The music thudded so loud it could be heard for two miles over the engine of a Ford Model T. And Becky Mackenzie was right smack in the middle of all of it.

After her fourth dance partner for the evening, she flopped back into her seat at the round table in front of a high-backed booth and sipped from someone's champagne glass before patting her forehead with a linen napkin. She smiled, waved, and then leaned over to her best friend, Martha Bourdeaux, to talk directly in her ear.

"Give me a ciggy," she said.

"Am I seeing things, or are you and Fanny getting along better these days?" Martha asked as she pulled a cigarette from her clutch purse.

Becky wrinkled her nose before popping the cigarette into her mouth and striking a match. "I wouldn't say we are getting along." She inhaled and blew the smoke up into the air. "I'm just trying to make my mother happy. She insists Fanny is depressed about leaving Paris."

"She doesn't look depressed." Martha jerked her chin in Fanny's direction.

Cousin Fanny had come to visit the Mackenzie tobacco plantation after visiting Grammy Louise in Europe, mostly France. At this moment, she was standing at the long bar with three gents around her ready to do her bidding for a taste of gin from her slipper.

"No, she doesn't," Becky said. "She shouldn't. Mama just bought her that new dress today to help get her out of the doldrums." She shook her head and took another sip of champagne. "Is this my drink?"

"It is now," Martha replied, giggling.

"Hello, girls!" came a female voice from somewhere inside the dancing mob. "Woohoo! Over here!"

Becky and Martha saw a waving hand in a long black glove with a bucket of ice around the wrist.

"That's got to be Violet," Martha said, laughing.

"Of course it is. Who else has that kind of jewelry in this place?" They waved and smiled back, urging the young woman to come join them.

Violet Darcy couldn't help but slink when she walked. Her hourglass figure wouldn't allow for anything else, and there wasn't a gent in the joint who didn't take notice. It would have been easy to hate her, except she had a heart of gold that shined through her smile and twinkling green eyes. Becky and Martha had known her since childhood. Unlike them, Violet had grown up on a piece of land that produced nothing but more siblings. She was somewhere in the middle of nine children at last count but hadn't gone back to her family homestead in years. A father who drank and a mother who all but gave up on life were too much for the raven-haired beauty to endure. She wanted more and used the only thing she had to get it.

"I haven't seen you both in ages!" Violet said over the music. Her long hair hung in lavish finger waves across the left side of her face and down to her shoulders. "How's tricks?"

"Can't complain." Becky took Violet's gloved hand in hers to inspect the ring of diamonds around it. "Was it your birthday? How do you even lift your hand?"

"It was a gift from Leonard." She blushed and looked at her wrist. That was when her hair fell forward, revealing the deep purple shiner over her left eye.

"Great balls of fire, Violet! What happened?" Becky asked, her eyes wide with concern. "Your eye! Does it hurt? You poor thing."

"Oh, you know me. Had a little too much champagne and walked into a door. It's nothing." She smiled as if she believed her own lie.

Everyone knew what kind of guy Leonard was. He was a wise guy and a Bruno who had no problem putting people in their place if he felt they needed it. And the rumor was he felt almost everyone needed it. He towered over Violet by at least a foot and was built like the Farmall tractor Judge Mackenzie used every spring to till his land. This wasn't the first time Violet had shown up at a joint with a black-and-blue love tap from the guy. It usually led to another string of pearls, another sparkling pair of earrings, or another fur. She was the most glamorously dressed punching bag in all of Savannah.

"Pull up a chair, Violet. Have a drink with us," Martha urged, patting the empty spot next to her. "We were just about to get the boys to order up another round."

"I'd love to," Violet said before turning around and looking across the room. But just as she was about to slide behind the table, Leonard showed up and slipped his meaty paw around her tiny waist.

"Come on. We're going," he muttered.

"Oh, okay. Sorry, girls. Maybe next time?" Violet smiled and batted the one good eye that wasn't hidden by her hair.

"Absolutely!" Becky replied. "We'll save you a seat."

Violet waved and blew a kiss to Becky and Martha before turning her back and snuggling into Leonard's arm. Just as the diamonds on Violet's wrists sparkled and caused the ladies to look on with envy, Violet sparkled on Leonard's arm, making the men feel that same envy.

"She could do so much better," Martha snapped. "If Teddy ever thought he could sock me one, I'd pick up the heaviest thing I could get my hands on and give it right back."

"I know you would," Becky replied.

She watched them leave and felt a strange twinge in her stomach. Something wasn't right. Aside from the obvious—that Violet Darcy was a sweetheart of a gal mixed up with a real goon—something else had shifted in the air. Becky looked around and didn't see anything strange or out of place. She chalked it up to the *bad* that surrounded Leonard and let it go.

"Do you think she really loves him?" Martha asked.

"I do. I think she really loves Leonard and would do anything to prove it to him. And as crazy as this might sound, I think he loves her. As much as a gorilla like him could," Becky added. "But one thing is for sure. His way of showing that love is different from just about every other man in the world."

"Do you think she'll ever leave him?"

"I don't know. Violet would have to find herself the only guy in Savannah who was willing to cross not just Leonard but his *group of associates*, and those guys ain't much for being told what to do." Becky finished the glass of champagne in front of her.

"You aren't just whistling Dixie," Martha concurred.

"But I do pray she finds a fella like that. Someone who can take her away to start fresh. She's got such a good heart. It seems like a waste to give it to Leonard Brennan," Becky replied before waving to Teddy.

Theodore "Teddy" Rockdale was Becky's neighbor, Martha's main squeeze, and everyone's chauffer. His flivver could hold everyone if they all inhaled, and he was as charming behind the wheel as he was everywhere else. He waved back and hurried over.

"Bring us another round, would you, darling?" Becky batted her eyes.

"Absolutely." He leaned over and shouted in Martha's ear, "Please don't tell me your dance card is full!"

"I'd give them all the bum's rush for you, Theodore," Martha replied before giving him a quick peck on the cheek.

"Hot dog! Let me get you ladies a little more ambrosia, and we'll show them how it's done." Teddy turned on his heel and strutted back to the bar. He returned with a champagne cocktail in each hand and a shot of gin on top of his head.

"Your ability to stand upright is amazing," Becky

teased.

"I'm a man of many talents. Ready?" He extended his hand to Martha, who took a quick sip of her drink before accepting and letting him whirl her onto the dance floor, where they were all but swallowed by the crowd.

Becky was alone at the table. She'd danced with half the gents in the place already and chatted with their girls along the way. Every few seconds, someone new would wave hello to her or shout her name. Becky was popular and well-liked by just about all the regulars, with the exception of Cousin Fanny, who had an inherent dislike for anyone who was of the same gender as she.

As Becky looked around the room, she caught a glimpse of Violet slipping into a full-length fur, with Leonard watching everyone around. He wanted a girl who looked like Violet because it made him feel like a big shot. But Becky was sure that Leonard probably didn't even know how to spell her last name, as he wasn't all that interested in who she was but rather what she was. And what she was was the most beautiful arm ornament in Savannah.

Just as she was thinking this, she saw Leonard looking right at her. With a smirk, she raised her glass to him before taking a sip. He didn't show any emotion but instead leaned over to one of the goons sitting at the corner table in the shadows, jerked his thumb in Becky's direction, and whispered a few words. The other guy looked at Becky, who waved again. He didn't smile either but just nodded.

"What are you doing making eye contact with those kinds of men?" Fanny asked as she finally left the men at the bar and crashed down into the booth, bumping into her cousin. She was well lit and became even more annoying when she was.

"I've seen them around. They don't scare me," Becky said, still casually watching Leonard lead Violet out of the club, with two other men following close behind.

"They're gangsters. As sure as I'm sitting here," Fanny said. "And I don't know who that barlow thinks she is sashaying around showcasing those diamonds."

"Why, Fanny, don't tell me you're jealous of Violet," Becky poked.

"Jealous of her? I don't think so. I had plenty of fine beaus in Paris who were simply dying to drape me in jewels and finery. But Grammy Louise wouldn't hear of it. There's a name for girls who acquire their accessories that way," Fanny said.

"What is that name, Fanny?" Becky asked only

half listening.

"A belle-de-nuit. That's a woman of the night." She put her finger against her nose and looked at Becky seriously. "And if you aren't careful, well, birds of a feather. You know the saying."

That was the last thing Becky was worried about being called. Funny, the people she knew at all the speakeasies and juke joints would never think of her that way. But ask at her mother's beauty parlor or at the last Ladies' Auxiliary meeting, and they might say it was a distinct possibility.

The following morning, after a long night of dancing, Becky woke up with the sorest feet she'd ever had. As she tenderly walked barefoot downstairs, unsure how she was going to fit into her shoes, she heard her parents talking. There had been a murder.

"It says here she was last seen at a popular nightclub last night. My goodness, Judge, you don't think Becky could have known her?" Kitty Mackenzie asked as she rustled the newspaper.

"Knew who?" Becky asked as she winced and wiggled her toes when she entered the dining room.

"Morning, honey," Kitty said. "Paper says her name was Violet Darcy. Poor thing was found dead last night."

# CHAPTER TWO

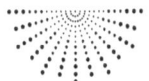

"*I* know the Darcys," Judge Mackenzie said before taking a sip of coffee. "A tragedy in that household. So many beautiful children, and a decent piece of land if the man had any desire to work it."

"Violet? Dead? What happened?" Becky snatched the paper away from her mother and quickly scanned the article.

"The article says she was found in the alley not far from where she lived. I find it interesting that a young lady, not married, could afford an apartment in that neighborhood." Kitty's back stiffened as she took a sip of coffee.

"Oh, Mama, Violet was a sweet girl. She didn't deserve this." Becky read the article, which said not much more than what her mother had relayed. "Oh my. This says she was shot. They suspect she was a casualty of rival gangs. I find that rather convenient."

"What do you mean?" Kitty asked. "Oh, Becky, I do hope that you aren't involved with such people. It doesn't take but once to be in the wrong place at the wrong time."

"Mama, I'm always in the wrong place at the wrong time. That's why I have so much fun."

Becky folded the newspaper and handed it back to Kitty. She sat down at the dining room table with her mind full of images of Violet, who she had just seen last night. The paper didn't mention the black eye. It also didn't mention whether any jewelry was found on her. Becky, knowing this wasn't just some accidental death, was sure someone had come along and taken the ice from around her neck and wrist. Probably Leonard himself, after he shot her. It would save him the trouble of buying Violet's replacement something new.

Becky finished her coffee and a hunk of cornbread before excusing herself.

"Where are you going?" Kitty asked.

"Well, it's a toss-up. I was thinking of either robbing the First Federal Bank of Savannah in the middle of town or going out to do some sketches of nature. Which do you think is more prudent?" Becky asked her mother seriously.

Judge chuckled behind the paper he'd snatched from Kitty.

"Don't you go on encouraging her. Rebecca Madeline, you are the thorn in my side." Kitty sighed.

"All right, Mama. For you, I'll stick to the right side of the law. I'll just be out and about drawing the lay of the land."

"Now you be back in time for lunch. We have a visitor joining us."

Those words froze Becky in her tracks. She shifted from one foot to the other and looked at her mother with her right eyebrow raised.

"Who is joining us for lunch?" Becky asked.

"His name is Roland P. Welch. He's a fine fellow. Kin to the Merriweathers on his grandmother's side. Now, he's a slight bit older than you, but maybe that is your dilemma. The young bucks around here are just too juvenile for you. A man with a bit more worldly experience might be just the ticket," Kitty said with a simper on her lips.

"Mama, you know I'm seeing Adam White. He's been nothing but a perfect gentleman every time he's set foot on this property," Becky huffed.

"He has. I just don't think you should limit your-self. The world is a big place, and Roland has seen quite a bit of it. He can show it to you. It's about time he settled down as well." Kitty said all this as if it made perfect sense.

Judge looked over his paper at her. "Kitty, how much older is this Roland P. Welch?" he asked.

"Oh, not much. Five, maybe ten years Becky's senior. Give or take a year or two," Kitty replied proudly.

"Mama, you are the thorn in my side," Becky huffed before heading upstairs to get her sketchbook and retreat to the Old Brick Cemetery that was behind the Mackenzie tobacco field.

Just as she was getting to her room, Cousin Fanny appeared from the water closet. She looked a little worse for wear, with dark circles under her eyes. But no one ever noticed her eyes when Fanny walked into a room. Today would be no different.

"Morning, Fanny," Becky said. "Feeling all right?"

"I'm just fine," she lied. "I hear you have a gentleman caller paying you a visit today."

"How do you know?"

"Aunt Kitty told me about it yesterday. I do believe she has a splendid idea, but I don't think a man that much your senior should be calling on you.

A man with experience doesn't have to be old. Like Stephen Penbroke." Fanny cleared her throat.

"Why would you bring him up?" Becky squinted at Fanny as if she might be able to catch a glimpse of her motive.

"I can't help it, Cousin Becky. I see something in the two of you. I know it isn't my place. I'm just being honest." Fanny smiled. "Well, I don't expect you to take my word for it. Just because I did successfully matchmake several of my acquaintances in Paris, who would have otherwise been roaming around lonesome and miserable for heaven knows how long, that doesn't give me any authority over your love life."

With that, she sashayed down the hallway and out of sight downstairs. Becky could hear her chirping a good morning to Kitty and Judge. She knew that Fanny had seen something the night that Stephen had been forced to stay overnight. Had she seen their kiss? Did she suspect? There was nothing to it. It meant nothing. She'd even told Adam about it, because it was nothing but horsefeathers. Had Stephen said something to Fanny? They always did seem to gravitate together.

"That's it." Becky snapped her fingers. "Fanny wants you interested in Stephen so she can yank him out from under you. Silly girl. Cousin Fanny Doshoffer doesn't have anyone but Cousin Fanny Doshoffer in mind when she does anything."

Becky shook off the conversation and went in her room to gather a few things in order to spend a comfortable afternoon away from her visitor, Roland P. Welch. But as she shimmied down the trellis, her plans of a quiet afternoon in the cemetery were quickly dashed.

"Miss Becky?" Teeter was standing at the bottom, his face screwed up with worry. Teeter was the only child of Moxley, the Mackenzie butler, and Lucretia, the head maidservant of the Mackenzie estate. They had been with the family for so long they were like family themselves. So when Teeter had a problem it wasn't something Becky could just ignore.

"Good morning, Teeter. What's got you in such a state?" Becky asked as the boy nervously kicked at the dirt with his bare feet. He had shoes. He just refused to ever wear them.

"Nothin'."

"Well, how about you walk with me and tell me all about that nothin'," Becky said, taking the boy by the hand. The cemetery would have to wait.

As it turned out, Teeter had a serious dilemma.

He'd lost his good-luck marble and was just beside himself. Becky told him that meant he was full of good luck and the marble had gone off to find someone else who needed good luck. It wasn't the greatest answer, but it was all she could come up with. However, by the time she got the story from Teeter and was able to convince him he'd not be overcome with bad luck, it was lunchtime. There was no escaping Roland P. Welch. He was already pulling up the driveway.

He arrived in a sleek flivver and was wearing aviator goggles and leather gloves. When he smiled, he showcased the most perfect set of teeth Becky had ever seen. His smile was surrounded by a peppered mustache, and his skin had been in the elements more than it had been indoors, resulting in a map of tan wrinkles. When he climbed out of his car, Roland revealed he was a mountain of a man, including the white on top, and it made Becky think Adam would have looked like a greenhorn if he'd been standing next to him.

"You must be Rebecca." He grinned as he approached, taking quick, long strides before catching Becky in a bear hug, sweeping her off her feet and twirling her around. "Why, you're as pretty as a daisy in May."

When he finally set her down, she had to catch her breath.

"Is that you, Mr. Welch?" Kitty called from inside the house.

"Why, yes, ma'am. The one and only." He smoothed his hair back as he climbed the porch steps. "Mrs. Kitty Mackenzie? I do appreciate your hospitality. I've heard nothing but good things from Ellen-Lyn."

"That would be a first," Becky muttered.

"And might I just say your daughter Rebecca is quite a sight." Roland winked.

Kitty smiled proudly, and Becky could tell from her face that her mother was already picking out a date on the calendar for a wedding.

"Mr. Welch, please come in," she said as she told him to call her Kitty and introduced Fanny, who Becky was sure had bolted from her room to the parlor in order to make a proper entrance. As Becky walked in behind Roland, she was shocked at his response to Fanny.

"It is my pleasure to make your acquaintance," Fanny cooed, flipping her blond hair and making sure he got an eyeful of every curve.

"Are you an actress?" Roland asked her point-blank.

"Why, no," Fanny replied.

"So you wear that much face powder all the time?" He winced as if Fanny had needles stuck in her eyelids.

"Well, I never—"

"Oh, I mean no disrespect," he said, standing tall and unapologetic. "It's just a man like me isn't used to seeing ladies so dolled up. You see, I just got back from spending three months climbing the Appalachian Mountains. Oh, it was magnificent. Before that, I had crossed Death Valley. The stars were my guides at night. I slept in a tent during the day. The heat was worse than the hottest corner of Hades. But what a journey."

"Mr. Welch, would you like a glass of lemonade?" Kitty asked.

"Why, that sounds absolutely splendid. And please, call me Rollie. Everyone does." He smiled that wide, toothy grin and looked down his barrel chest at Kitty before focusing his attention on Becky.

"Fine, Rollie. Fanny and I will get the refreshments while Becky escorts you to the parlor," Kitty replied.

Becky felt no attraction to Rollie, but she couldn't help being mesmerized by his personality. He was quite a character.

"Miss Becky, I want to know all about you. Tell me everything. Something says you've got quite a story to tell."

"Not really." Becky smiled as she took a seat in the armchair while Rollie sat directly across from her.

"Oh, come now. I'm sure you haven't jumped from an airplane like I have or swum among sharks, but..." Rollie smoothed his mustache before continuing. "Those are stunts better left for the stronger sex. I'd no more expect you to wrestle an alligator in order to get a new pair of boots than you'd expect me to... well... give birth to a baby." He laughed as he stretched out his long, thick legs, which ended in a pair of sharp, scaly alligator boots.

Becky folded her arms across her chest and watched as Rollie launched into the tale of how it was he had come to wrestle that alligator. He was a few minutes into the story when Judge appeared. Becky made all the proper introductions.

"Daddy, Rollie was just telling me about how he came to own those boots. He wrestled an actual gator for them." She nodded, smiling up at her father.

"Well, I'd say there has to be an easier way for a

man to get a pair of boots, Mr. Welch." Judge laughed.

Rollie did too.

And Becky found herself enjoying the stories Rollie had to tell. Even though he'd asked her to tell him about herself, he hadn't taken a breath long enough for her to get a word in.

Finally, it was lunchtime, and Rollie was still in the parlor entertaining everyone with his stories of adventure.

"Rollie, how about I sweeten that lemonade for you," Judge offered. "I've got some excellent bathtub gin in the cellar that I'd be happy to bring up. Or if champagne is more to your liking…"

"Never touch the stuff." For the first time all evening, Rollie's smile disappeared.

"Daddy does have some rye that is for those with a more developed palate," Becky offered, only to see Rollie visibly ruffle as if someone had walked across his grave.

"None of it. I won't taste a drop." He wouldn't budge.

Becky was ready to show him the door.

"Oh, and may I ask why that is?" Judge looked at his daughter, who stood with her mouth hanging open and her hand on her hip.

"You're an intelligent man, Judge. I'm sure you've seen more than your fair share of incidents that could all but be avoided had it not been for the parties involved imbibing to excess," Rollie lectured.

"I'm not talking about a bender, Rollie. I'm just offering you a cocktail." Judge smiled pleasantly.

"And if that isn't enough, it is against the law," Rollie said sternly.

"I do hope you're not going to turn us in," Judge said playfully.

"Not at all. What a man does on his property is his own business." He looked at Becky and took a deep breath. "Now, you distracted me with that red hair of yours, Rebecca. I do apologize. Please, you were going to tell me about yourself."

Becky looked at her father who raised his eyebrow before leaving the room.

"There isn't much to tell you about me. But there was some excitement we just learned about this morning," she said.

"Do go on." Rollie smiled and leaned forward.

"It's a rather gruesome story, but a woman I knew was just found dead this morning. Her body was discovered in an alley not far from her home. I had just seen her last night at Willie's speakeasy,"

Becky said and continued to talk about her suspicions regarding Leonard and his past behavior.

When she finally stopped and looked at Rollie, he'd gone pale in the face and stared at her.

"I'm thinking that this evening I might do a little snooping around. You'd be surprised at what people know after they've tossed back a few." Becky smiled and waited for the adventurer to ask to tag along. But she couldn't have been more wrong about him.

"I find it all rather gruesome," Fanny said as she came in the parlor. "The young lady who suffered this tragedy wasn't known to hang around with an honest crowd."

Becky wanted to tell Fanny to mind her own business, but what she'd said wasn't a lie.

"Fanny is right. She had a jealous boyfriend, and he had some suspicious characters as business associates. It's really sad." Becky shook her head.

"Am I to understand that you associate with these kinds of characters?" Rollie asked.

"There are all kinds of people that go to Willie's. The music is jumping, and the liquor is wet. What more could you ask for?" Becky smiled playfully. "In fact, I'm sure we'll be heading out to a juke joint tonight, Rollie. You are more than welcome to join us. I know my dear friend Martha would think you're the cat's pajamas. You've got to tell her the story about those boots. She'll swoon."

"I don't think that would be a good idea, Rebecca." Rollie stood up and smoothed out the front of his pants. "But I'm afraid I don't approve of that sort of establishment. Not for myself and not for a prospective fiancée."

Becky looked like she'd suddenly felt the snap of all the elastic in her pantaloons. With that, Roland P. Welch was out the door leaving nothing but the echo from his flivver to indicate he had even been at the house.

"Wait until Ellen-Lyn Merriweather hears about this." Fanny snickered.

"I don't know how I'll ever set foot in the beauty salon again," Becky replied before starting to chuckle.

# CHAPTER THREE

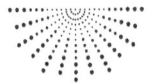

"*W*hen is your mother going to stop trying to get you married off?" Martha laughed over her gin rummy. "I thought Adam was a fairly familiar visitor at the Mackenzie plantation."

"He is. Sometimes," Becky said over the music. Teddy had driven them to a joint called The Clubhouse. It was nothing more than an empty basement at the bottom of an apartment building with a rickety piano playing nonstop. "She still hasn't warmed up to him."

"Well, there's no hurry," Martha said. "So, the story about poor Violet scared off Mr. Alligator Boots. I can't say I blame him. Can you believe we just saw her last night?"

"Yeah, and we saw what Leonard had done to her too. I'll bet my last dollar he's responsible. He killed her as sure as I'm sitting here," Becky said.

"You're that sure? I think it could have been him or any number of his goon friends," Martha said. "Let's face it. She wasn't your average beauty. Violet Darcy was perfection. I don't think it would be a stretch to say any of those guys might have put the moves on her and, rather than face Leonard, just got rid of the evidence."

"That could be. But Leonard never let her out of his sight. You saw how he was yesterday. None of his goons would have had any time to get her alone," Becky mused before taking a drink of her gin rummy.

"I don't think we should spend any more time dwelling on this." Martha scooted in her seat. "We've got two great gents ready to dance with us. Life is for the living." She patted Becky's arm and pointed to the door.

When she looked, Becky saw not the toothy smile of some wild adventurer but the handsome smile of Adam White. Suddenly, Becky felt warm all over. With a smirk on her lips, she pretended not to notice him and looked up at the ceiling and around at the piano player.

"I think they're playing our song," Adam said, his shirt sleeves rolled up tight around his bulging biceps. He placed his hands on the small table and leaned directly in front of Becky.

She looked up at him and smiled. Before her mind could even think, she was on her feet, in Adam's arms, and being whirled around the small dance floor as if she was as light as a feather. Adam was a good dancer. He knew all the latest steps and could carry on a conversation, whispering in Becky's ear until any song came to an end. Like he was doing now. Becky giggled at the things he was saying, but as they moved across the floor, easily maneuvering through the other dancers, Becky caught sight of another familiar face. Violet was across the room. She was standing in the pretty dress and long gloves she'd been wearing the previous night. Becky looked directly into both of her eyes. She could see them both. Her left eye was no longer a puffy, purple mass. She was whole. But she wasn't. She couldn't have been. She was dead.

No one else seemed to notice her. That was odd in itself, since she usually couldn't enter a room without every gent getting an eyeful. But yet people were walking past her, scooting around her, not like she was a physical obstacle to maneuver around but like she was a dark shadow or a cold draft to be avoided.

Adam squeezed Becky tighter, and she squeezed him back even though she was distracted. He continued to whisper in her ear, but she wasn't hearing everything he was saying. She absently nodded and agreed with him until she couldn't take it anymore.

"Excuse me, Adam. I have to powder my nose," she purred to him.

"Right now? I've been thinking about this moment all day, and you're going to make me wait?" He squeezed her again.

"I'll be right back." She kissed his cheek then pulled away from him. "You're wearing your work boots. You won't suffer any injuries if you give Fanny a spin around the floor."

"If you say so." Adam winked and looked around for Fanny, who was at the small bar with a fellow at each elbow. Most women would call Becky crazy to send Adam to a jackal like Fanny, who was all too happy to hang off his arm. But Becky didn't have time for petty jealousy. She was looking right at a dead woman, and that dead woman was turning and starting to walk away through the crowd and down a dark hallway. Still, no one saw Violet. Even as she swung her hips the way she'd done in life, there wasn't a pair of eyes on her except Becky's.

"Excuse me," Becky said, pushing past a group of dancers. "I'm sorry. Pardon me. Excuse me," she continued as she shoved her way through the crowd.

Just as she reached the hallway, she saw Violet take a turn to the left. Hurrying after her, Becky's only thought was that she knew what she was seeing wasn't real. It couldn't be. But Becky had this thing about seeing dead people, and, well, there had to be something to this.

For as long as Becky could remember, she'd had special friends, interesting characters in funny clothes or who spoke in old-time jargon coming up to her. They weren't scary specters that shook her bed or played tricks on her. They were regular people who talked to her and told her stories. Mostly they stayed within the confines of the Old Brick Cemetery, where Becky enjoyed spending time alone. But on a rare occasion, she'd be confronted in the world, like she was now.

"Violet!" she hissed down the hallway, hoping no one but the woman walking ahead of her would hear. "Violet! Is that you?"

Violet stopped before looking in Becky's direction. She had no expression on her face but stared as she continued and disappeared around the corner. Becky looked over her shoulder. No one was following her. She turned back and hurried in the direction Violet had gone. As soon as she rounded the corner, she saw Violet standing in front of an open door. There were brooms and buckets along the wall and a couple of dollies loaded with crates marked with the words GIN, VODKA, CHAMPAGNE.

Carefully, Becky tiptoed closer, only to have Violet walk silently into the room. Becky could hear voices. There were two men speaking. With her breath held in her chest, she inched closer, put her hand against the wall, leaned toward the door, and listened.

"I don't know what I'm going to do," one man said.

"What's done is done. You can't change that," the second man said. His voice was flinty, sharp like a baseball game announcer's.

"I loved her, Lou. I really did."

"What love? I can get you that kind of love from any girl in town," Lou replied.

Becky leaned forward, and through the crack between the door and door jamb, she saw Leonard talking with some small, wiry fella wearing his shirt collar open and a pinky ring the size of a half-dollar on his left hand.

Leonard chuckled. "Not that kind of love."

"Look, it had to be done. You might have been in love, Lenny, but she loved your money. Plain and simple. Now, you've got a job to do and—"

Becky nearly lost her balance and, in the process, grabbed onto a broom handle to steady herself, only to kick one of the metal buckets down the hallway, making enough racket to wake the dead. Leonard knew Becky from Willie's and a few other places, and whenever Violet talked to her, he had whisked her away. She didn't dare let him see her there eavesdropping. Without waiting, she darted around the corner and back down the hallway, where she grabbed the arm of the first fella she saw and dragged him onto the dance floor.

"Hi. I'm Becky. I just love this song, don't you?" she flirted.

"Sure do," the stranger replied as he proceeded to stomp on her feet. "I'm sorry. I'm not that good a dancer. But you sure are swell. What do you say we have a little kiss?" He leaned in with juicy, gin-soaked lips. Becky put her hand over his mouth.

"After the dance," she said before peeking over his shoulder.

Leonard was standing there, his hulking shoulders heaving with rage as he scanned the crowd for whoever had been listening to his conversation. Becky thought she was doing a fantastic job of hiding behind her dance partner, but as soon as Leonard saw her peeking over his shoulder, he glared at her. She saw his fists clench and the muscles in his jaws work up and down.

Becky pretended not to take notice, but her heart was thumping like the leg of a jackrabbit. Without even realizing it, she was squeezing her dance partner.

"My, you are friendly," he said. "How about we blow this pop stand and go for a drive?"

"Oh, no thanks. I just really liked this song." She pulled away. "You dance divinely," Becky said and hurried to her table, where Adam was watching her, his eyebrow raised and his arms across his chest.

"That corn shredder did a number on my toes. That's what I get for taking him at his word that he could dance," Becky fibbed as she made herself comfortable, squeezing tightly against Adam. "I'm thirsty. Where's my drink? Did you have a good day at work, darling? I missed you."

"You are up to something, Rebecca," Adam said.

"Oh, don't call me Rebecca. Don't ever call me

that." She shook her head, repeating the details of the afternoon's events. "You simply must come over more frequently, Adam. I know Daddy has already been taken by you, but Mama is as stubborn as a mule. She just needs a little more buttering up."

"Horsefeathers. That woman wouldn't like me if I was dipped in gold and branded with the Confederate flag," Adam replied. "But you think your Daddy is sold on me?"

"Abso-tively. A man who works hard is a man he can trust. Besides, he does not approve of my mother's attempts at matchmaking. He knows I will ultimately do what I want." She looked up at him dreamily.

"And what is it you want to do?" Adam asked, looking down at her.

"Just this," she said, kissing him on the lips.

For a moment, she'd forgotten about Violet and what she'd seen. Perhaps the word "forgotten" was the wrong term. She put it out of her mind for the moment and enjoyed the world stopping for those few seconds. But when she opened her eyes, even though she was looking up at Adam, she felt there were eyes staring at her, waiting to lock with hers so they could see guilt on her face. But she held fast, smiled at Adam, and listened to him as he and Teddy began a story. It was about some rummy at another juke joint and a banana peel and maybe a mouse. Becky wasn't sure. But when the punchline came, she acted as if it was the funniest thing she'd ever heard. And so things went on for a little longer until Fanny interrupted, pointing her finger and squealing with delight.

"Well, look what the cat dragged in. If it isn't Stephen Penbroke," she gushed.

Becky looked in the direction of the door and waved. Adam stood up to shake Stephen's hand, as did Teddy. He offered the man a seat and something wet.

"The gin is exceptionally cold tonight. I don't know what they did to the ice, but it goes down smooth," Becky said, patting him on the back.

"I should have known I'd find you here," Stephen said.

"Oh? Were you looking for me?"

"I always am," he said in her ear, just above a whisper.

Just then, Adam came back and handed him a glass with a clear liquid in it. They all toasted to Stephen—better late than never—and the jabbering continued.

"I know we aren't the only ones not surprised to

hear about Violet," Martha said. "She was such a sweetheart."

"I don't think we should talk about it here," Becky said out of the side of her mouth.

"Why not? Everyone knows it was that no-good palooka she was dating who did it." Martha looked at Becky. "We were just saying it last night, right, Beck?"

"We were," Becky said quietly while looking around to make sure no one was listening to their conversation who shouldn't have been. She couldn't help the feeling of dread inside her gut. The fact that everyone in the place had probably mentioned Violet Darcy at one point during the course of the night made no difference. Becky had heard what Leonard had said to that man, Lou. It was basically a confession that he'd killed her. And she'd heard him say it. Then, like a bulldog in a chicken coop, she'd bumped and bumbled around making enough noise for anyone to think the sky was literally falling.

"If I were to see that goon, I'd tell him to his big, flat face that I knew he did it and that I hope they strap him to Old Sparky once they catch him," Martha continued. She was working on her third gin rummy and feeling mighty brave.

"Easy does it, tiger," Teddy said.

"I think that we should all mind our own business," Adam added. "Violet was nice, I agree. But when you get involved with gangsters like that, well, there are only two ways things can end up. Either you're in for life or you're in for life."

"That is so profound." Martha stared at Adam before she was struck with the giggles.

"I think we ought to call it a night," Becky said.

"But I just got here," Stephen protested, raising his glass and tossing back the rest of his drink.

"If you want to go home, I'll drive you," Adam offered.

"That sounds swell," Becky said and, in a whirl, kissed Martha on the cheek and said good night to everyone else. Before her seat was even cool, Fanny had slithered in next to Stephen.

❧

*F*anny watched him as he watched Becky slip her hand in Adam's and walk out the door.

"You don't seem to be making much progress," Fanny said to Stephen. "Looks to me like Becky is more dedicated to Adam than ever."

"I don't know how they do things in Paris, Fanny,

but here in the States, slow and steady wins the race." Stephen cleared his throat and straightened his tie.

"Is that so?" she purred.

"You don't seem to have caught Adam's attention either. From where I'm sitting, you aren't doing much better."

"I don't have to do anything. A man can't live on bread alone. I just need to bide my time." She batted her lashes and pouted.

Had Stephen not learned what Fanny was all about, he would have been in hot pursuit of her. But while her greatest strength was that she was all woman, it was also her biggest weakness. And he wasn't interested in playing a game of chess for the rest of his life, constantly trying to guess the next move. He wanted Becky. And by hook or by crook, he was going to win her over.

If only he knew how close to Adam Becky was sitting as he drove her home, Stephen might have been more inclined to drop his whole pursuit.

"*T*ake the long way, Adam. I'm in no hurry," she said as she snuggled against his chest with his arm around her shoulder.

"I thought you wanted to get home," he said.

"I wanted to get out of there. I don't know if Martha was aware, but I saw Leonard Brennan in there. The guy gives me the heebie-jeebies. And you know what he did to Violet. You know she didn't get her bumps and bruises walking into any door or tripping while getting out of his car."

"I know, Becky, but I also know she was a grown woman who made her own decisions," Adam replied. "Trust me. It won't take long for Leonard to find another girl just like Violet. They come a dime a dozen."

"Ugh, the whole thing makes me climb the walls. I don't understand it. She could have had her pick of any guy, and she chose Leonard Brennan," Becky huffed. "Ick."

"Almost any guy," Adam replied as they got nearer to the Mackenzie plantation and the long dirt road that led to the front of the house. He pulled the car over and shut off the engine. The air smelled of the sweet tobacco plants, and a chorus of cicadas was chirping as the crescent moon hung high in the sky.

"What do you mean?" Becky asked.

"You don't think I'd ever want a girl like Violet Darcy, do you?" Adam pulled Becky closer to him. "She was nice and, yes, she was pretty, but, call me crazy, there was something wrong with her."

"Oh yeah? What?" Becky asked.

"She wasn't you," Adam replied.

Becky had thought about telling Adam about seeing Violet at the club. He knew she had the uncanny gift of seeing those that had passed on. But when he spoke such sweet words, when his lips felt so soft and his arms around her felt so strong, every thought in her head took to flight. She gently touched his cheek as they kissed once more before he brought her to the front door. Like a real Southern gentleman, Adam got her car door for her, walked her up the front porch steps, and stood there with his hands clasped behind his back.

"I had a wonderful evening, Becky. Do you think I could call on you later this week?"

"I'd be disappointed if you didn't." She stood on her tiptoes and gave him a long, loving kiss on the cheek before saying good night.

Once in the privacy of her room, out of her dress and in her nightclothes, Becky took her sketchbook and a pencil and started to draw. At first, she doodled random faces and bodies, but before she knew it, she was drawing Violet. Then, like a skip in a movie at the theater, Becky was drawing and then suddenly found herself sprawled out on the bed as if she'd passed out. Her hand was still holding the pencil. Her sketchbook had fallen to the floor. Without thinking, she pushed herself up onto her elbow and ran her hand through her loose red hair. It was as if she'd been slipped a mickey during the course of her evening out that had had a delayed reaction.

"What is going on?" She rubbed her face then reached down to pick up her sketchbook. When she looked at the page she'd been drawing on, she gasped. There was an address in scribbled letters with a heart shape. It was the last word that made Becky feel a cold chill across her back and shoulders. Beneath the heart was the signature... Violet.

## CHAPTER FOUR

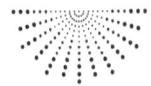

The next day, a trip to town with Moxley was all that was on Becky's mind.

"I wasn't planning on going downtown today, Miss Becky," Moxley said. "Why? Does your mama have another suitor fixing to pay you a visit?"

"I wouldn't be surprised, but as far as I know, today is a free day," Becky whispered. "Are you sure you don't have anything you need to pick up in town? Not a couple of screws at the hardware store or maybe some yarn for Lucretia's knitting?"

"Miss Becky, have you ever thought that maybe it's time you try your hand at driving again? You are a grown woman who—"

"I'll thank you, Moxley, for not bringing up my driving habits," Becky snapped, lifting her chin defiantly. The memory of her tragic first driving experience surfaced, making her blush and rapidly blink her eyes. "And I'll get behind the wheel again when I'm good and ready. Now, are you going to go downtown or not?"

Moxley chuckled as he walked into the kitchen with Becky close behind him. His wife, who was standing at the stove with her back to them both, was obviously trying not to laugh as well. But Becky knew she was, seeing her shoulders shaking.

"You, too, Lucretia?" Becky pouted as she put her hands on her hips.

"I'm sorry, Miss Becky," Lucretia said without turning around. "I'll stop." Of course, she didn't. "Moxley, I suppose I could use some molasses. And I was just telling Teeter that he had a hole in the knees of his newest britches already. If you could find me some brown thread."

"I still think Miss Becky could drive herself if she put her mind to it," Moxley teased. "Your daddy would forgive you if he saw—"

"I'll meet you out front" was all Becky said, not only at the house but for the entire trip. When she hopped out of the car, she looked at Moxley, who was still smiling. She grabbed her purse and started to walk off in a huff.

"Miss Becky, what time will you be finished with your errand?" He cleared his throat and stood up straight, looking at her seriously as if he were answering a drill sergeant.

Becky tried not to snicker, but it was impossible. Moxley knew how to make her laugh.

"I don't know when I'll be done. I'll take a cab home." She smirked.

"All right, then, Miss Becky. See you at home," Moxley said and left for the general store just a few blocks away.

Becky turned on her heel and started to walk in the direction of the address she'd scribbled the night before.

1970 East Erie Street. This was a nice part of town. It certainly wasn't the ritziest, but if Becky had a desire to live in the city, she could do a lot worse than this address. The building she was looking for was a sleek place with a revolving door, elegant sconces on either side of the entrance, and a red awning with the numbers 1-9-7-0 printed on it.

After taking a deep breath, Becky walked inside as if she knew exactly where she was going. If there was a doorman, he was not at his post. Without waiting to be questioned, Becky quickly walked to the elevator bank and hit the UP button. With a pleasant ping, the doors slid open, and she stepped inside. Just as the doors were sliding shut, a doorman appeared, adjusting his jacket and tugging at his sleeves. He didn't see her at all.

Once she was in the clear, Becky let out her breath and looked at the paper she had written the address on. She was looking for apartment 9D. When the elevator doors opened on the ninth floor, she carefully stepped out and listened. There was not a sound coming from any of the other apartments. Everyone else was either at work or asleep, Becky thought. Apartment 9D was at the very end of the hallway. She reached out and tried the knob, but the door was locked.

"How hard can this be?" she muttered while pulling a bobby pin from her hair. Quickly, she looked over her shoulder and confirmed she was still quite alone. Casually, she thrust the hairpin into the lock and began to jimmy it in any way that might slip the lock out of place. It felt as if she stood there for hours.

"I ain't no safecracker, and this ain't no box job," she mumbled as she became more and more frustrated. "What am I doing trying to bust into this place? What if it's a setup? I could end up in the hoosegow on a long stint for breaking into a dead woman's apartment. Why am I even doing this? Just because I had a dream and wrote down this address? Who knows? Maybe Teddy mentioned this part of town, or I overheard it at Willie's and it just stuck in my brain. This could be nothing…"

Just then, the lock clicked. Becky froze as if someone had stuck a rod in the middle of her back. With trembling hands, she reached up, took hold of the knob, and gave it a turn. It opened easily.

Quickly, Becky slipped inside, shut the door behind her, and snapped the button on the door-knob to lock herself in. When she turned around, she was not surprised at how amazed she was by Violet's apartment.

A bouquet of a dozen roses was dying in a vase on the dining room table. The other furniture—a chaise lounge, a loveseat, two armchairs, and a coffee table—was all expensive and shiny as if it hadn't ever been sat on. The ashtrays proved people had been there, though, and at least one of them had worn lipstick. There was a phonograph and lots of records. A rolling bar cart stocked with liquor sat invitingly next to the phonograph. The sheer curtains barely kept the light out.

Becky slowly walked toward the bedroom. There was one large bed with a frilly comforter and lots of pillows covered in silk cases. The closet door was open. Becky couldn't help but peek inside. Violet had more clothes than she could wear in a year and shoes to match. There was a champagne bucket with an empty bottle upside down inside it. Next to the bed sat two empty glasses on the nightstand. A gentle breeze disturbed the sheer curtain, making Becky jump. As she let out her breath, she saw the only shadow outside the window was the fire escape.

"My gosh. What a louse. He romanced her right before he killed her." Becky shook her head and grimaced. She walked over to the vanity. The three mirrors had allowed Violet to see her hair from all angles. The pieces of jewelry lying out represented a small fortune. Becky remembered seeing Violet wearing some of them. The face powder and lipstick were a fancy brand Becky had seen at the cosmetics counters when she shopped with her mother. A crystal ashtray held a couple of stamped-out butts. But the thing that caught Becky's eye was the ugly little book of matches next to it. When she opened it, she found an address written in it.

A gold cigarette case also sat there. Becky picked it up, snapped it open, and took one of the cigarettes from it. Before putting it back where she'd found it, she struck one of the matches from the book with the address written on it and lit the tip. After a long drag, Becky felt her nerves finally calming down. But it was short-lived, because she heard male voices at the front door.

Panicking, Becky slipped the matches into her pocket and looked around the room for a place to hide, but there was nothing. Under the bed? That would be the first place they'd look if not the closet. The vanity stood on long legs that provided no cover, and it was too late to dash to the other end of the apartment and hope for better hiding grounds in the kitchen. The only other thing was the window.

Quickly, with the cigarette still in her mouth, Becky dashed to the window. With both hands, she pushed it up just enough that she could wiggle through. The rusty bars of the fire escape were not accommodating her heels very well, making her lose her balance before latching on to the railing. She managed to maneuver herself to a position right next to the window. She pressed her body flat and waited.

"You don't have any idea what she did with it?" one male voice asked.

"I told her to hide it until I asked for it," the second voice replied.

Becky was sure it was Leonard, the same voice she heard the night before.

"You didn't think to ask her where she put it?" The other voice sounded annoyed.

"Look, Sam, Violet did as she was told. I didn't know things were going to turn out this way. It just sort of happened. Now, if you can quit flapping your gums and help me find it—"

"Yeah, yeah, yeah. I got it, Lenny."

Becky had been right. It was Leonard Brennan and some chump named Sam.

She heard their footsteps stomping up and down the floor. Drawers were being yanked open and dumped. All of Violet's pretty things were being tossed aside just as she had been. Becky took a puff from her cigarette and angrily exhaled the smoke.

"Someone's been here," Sam said.

"What are you talking about?" Leonard asked. "The door was locked."

Becky froze. Just then she took notice of the smoke rising from her cigarette. She snatched it from her mouth and flicked it over the edge of the fire escape platform.

"You smell that smoke? Someone was smoking in here," Sam said.

"Of course it smells like smoke. Violet smoked. I

smoke. Everyone who set foot in this apartment
smoked. Come on. We don't have time for this,"
Leonard said as he continued to rummage through
Violet's things.

"How big is it?" Sam asked.

"I don't know. Flask size. Small enough for her to
keep it under her skirt," Leonard replied, sounding
more than annoyed with his partner, Sam, who
made the mistake of speaking again.

"Lucky flask."

"Watch it. I'll bust you in the chops if you say one
more word," Leonard hissed.

"All right, all right. Sorry, Lenny. Sorry," Sam
stuttered. "I'll keep looking. No more talking. Just
looking."

Slowly, Becky let out her breath. The men went
back to the living room and continued shuffling
around. They started to speak, but Becky couldn't
hear, so she leaned closer to the window. Her heel
slipped through the grate, making her lose her
balance and kick over a stack of three terra-cotta
planters. They just rolled over onto the grate, but
Becky was sure it sounded as if a bull had just
destroyed a china shop.

Before she could think, she saw a small bundle
wrapped in brown paper and tied with a strand of

red yarn like a present. Becky stooped, picked it up, and dropped it into her pocket along with the ugly matchbook. She held her breath and pressed herself into the bricks.

From where she was standing, she could see clearly into the apartment directly across the alley. Random articles of clothing hung from the fire escape balconies. Other platforms had wooden crates as seating or tomato plants growing out of old dented pots.

"It's got to be here." Leonard was getting angry.

"You're sure she wouldn't have given it to someone to hold for her?" Sam asked.

"Like who? I was with her almost all the time," Leonard snapped.

"Well, not all the time, or else you would know where she hid it," Sam replied.

Becky shook her head, thinking Sam wasn't the brightest bulb on the tree.

"What did you just say?" Leonard barked. "I ought to snap your neck and toss you out that fire escape."

"I didn't mean anything by it, Lenny," Sam whined. "I'm just talking crazy. Making noise just to make noise. Honest. I didn't mean nothin' by it."

"Keep looking, and keep your mouth shut," Leonard hissed.

Becky heard his steps come closer to the window. Then she heard something that made her blood run cold.

"Violet? What are you doing?" It was the soft voice of a female. "Get back inside. It's dangerous to stand on the fire escape."

Becky turned her head and saw an older woman with a turquoise turban on her head and long false eyelashes leaning out of her window. She was squinting as she stared.

"Violet? Are you all right? Are you hiding from that man? I told you he was no good for you. But you never listened. You need to be careful out here. Go on back inside. Go on, now."

"I'll go in in a minute," Becky whispered.

"What? Violet, I can't hear you! Now stop playing games and get inside your apartment, or I'll call the police again!" the nosy neighbor shouted.

Becky heard the footsteps inside the apartment race to the window. When she turned to look, she only saw the beautiful face of Violet Darcy. All the wind was knocked out of Becky's lungs. Her mouth fell open, and a cry of surprise and fear echoed down the alley.

"Run!" Violet whispered before disappearing into thin air.

Becky stood there for a second before the movement behind the window snapped her into action. She turned and ran, as fast as her heels would allow, down the rusty, creaky, and wobbly fire escape steps. She tried not to see the long way down to the ground that was making her lose her balance and slow her steps. She was sure Leonard and his goon were closing in on her. But when she turned to look over her shoulder, she saw that Violet's bedroom window would not open wide enough for someone Leonard's size to get out. He had one leg out and was trying to raise the window with his shoulder to no avail.

Becky kept going and was two platforms away from the ladder that would get her to the safety of the sidewalk when she heard a loud crash. Looking up, she saw Leonard barreling down the fire escape two steps at a time. He was coming after her.

Without thinking, Becky pulled off her shoes and dropped them over the railing to the sidewalk below. Then, with as much resilience as she could muster, she focused only on the steps and not the cold, hard concrete littered with garbage and cigarette butts, where Violet had spent her final moments.

"Don't think about it, Becky," she muttered as she hurried down the steps, the rusty metal grates biting into her stocking feet. "Just don't think about it."

But the more she tried to tell herself not to think of Violet's body lying on the pavement, the more clearly the image came into view. There she was, lying just steps from the back door, her pretty dress ruined, her sparkling jewelry still around her neck and wrist, and a red halo spreading out from her hair where the bullet had exited her head.

Becky froze, her sweaty hands clinging to the railing as she leaned over like a person who had had one too many gin rummies. Above her, Leonard sounded as if he was having the same amount of trouble maneuvering the steps. Did he see what Becky was seeing? Did he see Violet's lifeless body lying on the ground?

When she looked up, she saw him staring past her toward the ground. He did see it, but it didn't stop him. His eyes snapped to Becky, and he snarled with anger, his face purple with rage and fear. It was now or never.

Without thinking, Becky sprinted down the last flight of rusty metal steps. By now, her feet were stinging with each step, and her breath was hitching in her chest. She was drenched in sweat. Her stockings were shredded. But once she reached the last landing, she took hold of the ladder and gave it a good, strong yank, sending it plummeting to the sidewalk. A couple bystanders stopped to watch as she shimmied down as if the devil was chasing her. If it wasn't the devil, it was a close associate.

The bars hurt her feet even more than the steps had, but there was no stopping now. Once at the bottom, Becky gave the ladder another push, sending it back up into the first-floor landing. She didn't want Leonard to have even a second of time to catch up to her.

"Are you all right, miss?" a fellow in a white apron asked. He had stepped out of the bistro next door.

"I am. But I think the guy behind me is having some kind of bad reaction. You may want to help him," she said as she scooped up her shoes. "He wouldn't let me do it. I think he's a dope fiend." And with that, she hurried in the direction of Erie Street, hopping as she slipped her shoes back onto her sore and swollen feet.

# CHAPTER FIVE

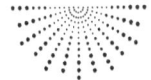

The sidewalk was a bit livelier, and Becky hurried to blend in with the crowd. Leonard wouldn't dare try to abscond with her in broad daylight, would he? One heard stories of wise guys committing crimes in the middle of the day—a shooting or bank robbery—while people were going about their business. Something told Becky that Leonard wasn't high enough on the food chain to pull off such a caper, but she wasn't going to loiter around and take that chance.

She needed a cab and fast. Her feet were on fire. It was bad enough that her shoes were digging into her heels and pinching her toes, but walking on those rusty metal grates had torn up the soles of her feet. She had no doubt she was hobbling along like a crippled person.

Suddenly, as Becky was imagining a thousand different ways Leonard was going to catch up to her, she heard the mad honking of a horn and a high-pitched whistle. If Leonard Brennan thought he'd get her attention that way, he was sorely mistaken. Still, the horn kept honking, and the catcall whistle continued. It couldn't be for her. Those kinds of whistles came when she walked past construction sites or maybe Fire Station No. 9, when the boys were sitting outside enjoying the cool night air.

"Becky! Hey, Becky! Where are you going?"

The voice was familiar. Becky turned around and had never been so glad to see Stephen Penbroke in her whole life. She smiled, dashed to his car, hopped in, and gave him a peck on the cheek.

"Make tracks, Stephen. We need to get out of here," Becky said as she turned around in her seat and looked for any sign of Leonard or his accomplice, Sam, who might be in pursuit.

The package in her pocket peeked out. Before she could conceal it, Stephen asked after it.

"Okay, but tell me what's in your pocket." He hit the gas, honking the horn, making a regular spectacle out of their departure.

"My gosh, do you want to attract the attention of every person in the neighborhood?" Becky squawked.

"You said get going. Sometimes people need a little push." Stephen smiled slyly as he shifted gears and hit the gas again. "Now tell me, what's in the box?"

"It's nothing."

"Becky, I saw you dart out of that alley. It isn't hard to see your stockings are all ripped, and you look like you just ran a marathon. Now, do you want to start from the beginning?"

There was no way Becky was going to tell Stephen what she was really up to. He wasn't like Adam, who knew there was no telling her what to do. He would try and scold her or shame her or even ridicule her for trying to get involved in a murder that had nothing to do with her. But it did. Violet had been such a nice person. And everyone knew already who the guilty party was. Everyone. To pretend there was another culprit was ludicrous.

"If I tell you, you can't breathe a word of it to anyone," Becky said as they made a hairpin turn around a corner.

"Cross my heart," Stephen replied.

Becky took a deep breath, put her hand on the

little package in her pocket, and finally looked at Stephen as he drove.

"I was running rum, and a beat copper almost caught me." It was the first thing to pop into her head. "I guess I'm not as good at it as I thought I'd be." She shrugged, smiled, and managed to blush a little.

"Rebecca Madeline Mackenzie, are you crazy? What will you do if Kitty or Judge have to come and bail you out of the hoosegow?" Stephen gasped.

"Are you for real? I couldn't tell you how many times my father had the police show up at our house for parties that got out of hand. He's seen people get arrested on more than one occasion for worse offenses." She cleared her throat and sat up straight in the seat.

"Yes, but they weren't his one and only child," Stephen said. "I think you are asking for trouble. Does Adam know?"

Becky looked at Stephen. Her eyebrows furrowed, shadowing her eyes, and her lip curled. This line of questions didn't sit well in her gut. Who the heck was Stephen to ask what Adam knew or didn't know?

"No," she snapped. Even though the whole thing was made up and she was no more a rum runner than the pope in Rome, she couldn't help feeling that Stephen was pulling rank on her by asking.

"I don't think he'd be very pleased," Stephen said. "But then again, I don't know the gent very well. Maybe he'd like it just fine."

"What are you trying to do, Stephen Penbroke? Are you looking for a sock in the puss or what?" Becky huffed. "I'm not handcuffed to you or Adam, and until that day comes, both of you can mind your own beeswax."

"You aren't honestly getting mad at me for caring, are you?" Stephen asked.

"Caring? Sounds more like controlling. I managed to make it twenty-three years without you, Stephen. I'm pretty sure I'd survive another twenty-three years on my own." She folded her arms while she stared out the windshield, her lips tightly compressed.

"Becky, the last thing any man who has known you for five minutes should ever try and do is control you." Stephen chuckled. "I think I've earned my place among your circle of friends and feel I can be honest with you. Am I wrong?"

Becky looked defiantly to the right.

"Now come on. After that sweet private moment we shared that night in your family's guest bedroom? Remember when we had to pull the wool over your parents' eyes in order to explain why you were in such a state? You do remember that, don't you?"

Becky's cheeks flushed. How dare he bring up that moment! She'd tried to put it out of her head, but here it was, right in the middle like a hound dog with fleas at a church picnic.

"I remember," she replied. "And when you describe it like that, it sounds much more torrid than it was."

"What?" Stephen's jaw dropped as he grinned. "Torrid?"

"It was a simple kiss, nothing more. And you know how much I appreciated your help that evening. I said as much. But let's not go pretending it was some kind of blood sacrifice that unites us for all eternity."

"It doesn't?" Stephen asked with that sly smile that Becky found disturbingly adorable.

"No, it doesn't."

"But you haven't forgotten," he continued.

"Forgotten what?"

"The kiss," he said and seemed to enjoy watching Becky's cheeks turn red all over again.

Becky took a deep breath and let out a groan.

"No, I haven't forgotten, because that was a very dangerous night, and you don't even know the half of it. I was desperate. I wouldn't have been able to explain to my parents anything that was going on, so you really came through. A peck on the cheek was the least I could do."

"Oh really? Do tell," Stephen teased.

"Now stop that." She slapped his arm playfully.

"Becky, when are you going to admit that you like me?"

"Of course I like you. You're a swell gent," she replied without looking at him.

"That isn't what I mean," Stephen pursued. "There was something in that kiss. You can deny it all you want, but I know there was. And I'll wait until the opportunity presents itself for us to do it again."

"You have lost your marbles," Becky said. "And why are you driving around the block a hundred times? If you aren't going to drive me home, I'll just get out and walk."

"Settle down, Rebecca." Stephen gently touched her arm. "I'll drive you back to the plantation. It seems I'm always around when you need to get back home."

Becky rolled her eyes at him and was glad he

didn't make her walk. Her feet were so happy to not be underneath her. If she were to put the slightest bit of weight on them, she was sure she'd fall flat on her face. As much as she wanted to focus on her sore toes, she felt Stephen's words stick in her head. That time they'd kissed seemed like forever ago. It had been a simple peck like she might give Teddy on Christmas Eve.

*Go ahead and tell yourself that, but you know it was a little more.* Her heart fluttered at the thought. *It might have been quick, but it was anything but simple.*

She licked her lips and stared out the windshield. She'd never tell Stephen or anyone that the kiss had been nice. Nor would she ever even whisper the fact that it had crossed her mind a couple of times. Even her best friend, Martha, didn't know about the kiss, nor would she ever. It was something she'd take to the grave, a guilty pleasure to relive when she was feeling down or needed a boost to her ego. It was not something to be taken seriously.

*Is Adam not enough to boost your ego? Is it the fact that he has a Northern accent? Maybe it's because his hands are stained with ink or that the dressiest thing he owns is a pair of brown slacks and a white shirt with a tie that is frayed at the end.* Her conscience was chiding.

*No! It's none of those things. I love Adam. He's differ-*

*ent, and he understands me, and he's the best-looking fella in all Savannah.* She continued to argue internally while Stephen whistled as he drove down the long dirt road that led to the Mackenzie plantation.

As if she didn't have enough to keep her confused for days, as soon as they pulled up, Becky knew something was happening. Moxley was putting a suitcase in the car as it idled in front of the house.

Becky pulled off her shoes and inspected her feet before she stepped out of the car. Without a second thought, she hiked up her skirt and snapped her garters in order to pull off the rags that were the remains of her stockings.

Stephen let out a long whistle.

"Oh, I've had enough of you," Becky said without even looking at him.

"Come on, Beck. Okay, I won't say anything more about it. But I don't think I'd be under your skin if there wasn't just a little something to what I'm saying."

"You won't say anything more because there is nothing more to say. Now dummy up and don't go upsetting my parents," Becky ordered.

"Why would I upset your parents?" Stephen shrugged.

"The same reason you upset me. For kicks,"

Becky replied as she got out of the car and slammed the door shut.

As she went up the porch steps, she could hear her mother.

"I just don't know if I should leave you this way," Kitty said.

Becky hurried inside and saw Kitty with tears in her eyes, standing in front of Judge.

## CHAPTER SIX

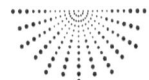

"What's going on?" Becky asked as she stepped into the foyer. While she stood there, Stephen came up behind her, letting himself inside.

"Your mother is having an episode," Judge replied.

"Mama, what's the matter?" Becky padded over to her, suddenly unaware of the sad state her toes were in.

"Now, Judge, don't make fun. I'll be so worried about you while I'm gone. We've not been apart for longer than a day or two since that glorious day we tied the knot," Kitty whimpered. "Becky, I'm going to need you to take care of your father while I'm gone."

"Where are you going?" Becky fretted.

"Oh, Becky, dear. I don't know how to tell you this. Your Aunt Hortense is dying," Kitty said as she took hold of her daughter's wrist. "I must go to Mobile and tend to her. Now, don't you fret. Alabama isn't that far. I'll be home as quickly as possible."

"She's still alive?" Becky wrinkled her nose.

"That's exactly what I said," Judge replied, rocking back and forth on his heels and crossing his arms over his chest.

"Yes, she's still alive, but we don't know for how long, and Carl says he can't take care of her and plan a wedding at the same time," Kitty replied.

"Who is getting married?" Becky asked.

"Carl is," Judge added.

"Her son Carl? Aunt Hortense is a hundred years old. Carl has got to be seventy-five if he's a day, and now he's getting married?" Becky couldn't suppress the snicker on her lips. She looked at her father, who was squeezing his eyes shut, quietly chuckling.

"Oh, he isn't that old. And neither is your aunt," Kitty said.

"Well, they certainly look it," Becky replied. "What about Aunt Tilly or Aunt Mimi? They live closer. Why don't they go and help her?"

"Because your Aunt Hortense told Aunt Tilly her

husband was cheating on her with one of the ladies in their church congregation who was blind in one eye and had a limp," Kitty replied.

"Well, was he?" Becky asked, looking at Stephen as if he were standing on his head.

"Yes, but no one wants to be told in such a crude manner," Kitty huffed.

"And what about Aunt Mimi?" Becky continued.

"Aunt Hortense told her her children were ugly, ill-behaved little monsters. And that is true too, I'm afraid. But then she threatened to lock them in the fruit cellar along with Carl's fiancée. It turned into a huge mess." Kitty waved the conversation away as if she were shooing a fly. "So you see, there isn't anyone else to tend to her in her final days. She needs me."

"It's all right, Mama. I'll take care of Daddy while you're gone. I'll make sure he doesn't have a lick of fun. Do you know when you'll be back?"

"I guess when she's dead." Kitty shrugged.

"Is she that close to the Pearly Gates?" Judge asked.

"I'm sure I don't know. I'll send word as soon as I assess the situation," Kitty replied. "You know, you could come with me. The men can handle the fields for a week or two."

"And spend that time in Hortense's big house that looks as haunted as Becky's Old Brick Cemetery? No thank you." Judge shivered.

"Hey, don't make fun of my cemetery." Becky frowned.

"My heavens! Becky, what happened to your feet? My darling, it looks like you ran barefoot through a briar patch." Kitty gasped.

"It's my fault, Miss Kitty." Stephen stepped in before Becky could come up with a convincing lie. "I ran into Becky downtown and made her run with me to the bursar's office that was closing in a matter of minutes. You see, my Aunt Ellen-Lyn asked me to run the errand for her. I didn't even know she had anyone attending university. But poor Becky was wearing such pretty shoes I should have known they would cause more pain than demonstrate any practicality."

"My goodness, you march yourself upstairs and have Dolores run you a hot soak for those." Kitty pointed to Becky's feet.

Before she could take a tender step, Fanny appeared, carrying a small suitcase. Could it be that Fanny was going with Kitty?

"Here you go, Aunt Kitty. Now don't you worry about us. I'll make sure that Judge and Becky eat their vegetables and get plenty of sleep." Fanny looked at Stephen as if he was a side of beef on sale at the butcher shop. "Why, hello, Stephen Penbroke. What a pleasant surprise."

Becky rolled her eyes and stepped closer to her father.

"Thank you, Fanny." Kitty took the small suitcase in her hands. "Stephen, I'm glad you're here. I'm sure you've heard that poor girl was found dead just the other day. My daughter said she knew her, and maybe you did as well."

"I'd seen her around." Stephen nodded.

"She had some questionable taste in companions. Always on the arm of a butter-and-egg man," Fanny added shaking her head and clicking her tongue. "There were a few times in Paris when I saw the same kind of gents. Sharp dressers and always throwing money around. Just a little common sense told any girl of class to stay clear of such men. But they always had girls like Violet around them."

"Well, I'd be much obliged if you'd stick by Becky's side if she insists on going out every night. That would put my mind at ease while I'm tending the deathbed of Aunt Hortense," Kitty replied, looking to Judge for approval.

"Mama, I am fully capable of taking care of

myself," Becky protested. "I don't associate with fellas who go off the tracks."

"I think that's a fine idea," Judge added. "And with Fanny along, well, there is power in numbers. I concur."

"Of course, I will, Mrs. Mackenzie." Stephen smiled at Kitty and quickly gave Fanny a wink before looking at Becky. "It would be my pleasure. So, will we be going out this evening?"

"My feet hurt," Becky replied.

With that, Kitty finished by blathering a few quick instructions, fussed over Becky and Fanny to be careful, kissed them both, thanked Stephen for his kind assistance, and finally looked to Judge. He took her small suitcase from her as he walked her to the car, where Moxley was waiting to take her to the train station.

"Are you sure you'll be all right?" she asked as they stepped onto the porch.

"Kitty, I've got Becky, Fanny, Lucretia, Dolores, and Moxley. I do believe I will survive," Judge said. "But do hurry back."

Becky smiled at her parents as she watched them say their goodbyes. As she peeked, she saw Kitty start to laugh. Judge had probably said something personal and off-color to make her chuckle that way.

It was not often that Kitty Mackenzie lost her head, but when she did it was always Judge Mackenzie's fault.

Without saying a word to Fanny or Stephen, Becky headed toward the stairs.

"Where are you going?" Fanny asked. "We have a guest."

"I'm sure you can entertain my babysitter while I go soak my feet," Becky answered. "And don't think for one second that I need a fire extinguisher when I go out. I never needed a chaperone before, and I'm not about to start now."

Without looking back, Becky strutted out of the foyer and up the stairs and locked herself in the bathroom. After turning on the water, getting a cool temperature, and filling the tub, she stuck her feet in the water. It was heaven. With soap lathered in her hand, she washed the dirt away and soothed the blisters that had developed.

But before she dried her toes and went to her room, Becky withdrew the treasures she'd collected at Violet's apartment. Neither one of them made much sense.

First, she studied the ugly little matchbook. It was worn around the edges, and a couple of matches were missing. It was an ugly brown color without any name or stamp on it. But it was the address scribbled on the inside that stuck with Becky.

"401 Portage Street." She chewed her bottom lip. "Why is that so familiar?" She shook her head and set the matchbook down. Then she took out the small package that was wrapped in brown paper with a piece of red yarn tied around it in a bow. It was like a Christmas present. Becky inspected it before opening. There was no name or marking on it. Carefully, she plucked the bow to unravel the yarn and unwrapped the object.

"Well, this is ducky," she said, holding the object in her hand. "A flask. Guess I really was rum running."

It was indeed just a simple silver flask that Becky could tuck into her garter belt for easy transport. She shook it, but it was empty. Looking it over, she found an engraving at the bottom: *LB Forever yours, VD.* This had to be what Leonard and Sam had been tearing Violet's place apart for. But if this had been a gift for him, why didn't he have it? Unless there was someone else with the initials LB. Becky couldn't imagine how big the guy would have to be to be brave enough to sweet-talk Violet. It wasn't as if people didn't know Violet was Leonard Brennan's squeeze. He made sure everyone knew. But the flask had been on the fire escape, tucked inside an old planter. Why would she have put that there unless she was hiding it? How did Leonard know about it? Why had Leonard been tearing the place up for it?

Becky wrapped it back up and decided not to think about any of it for the rest of the day. She'd think about it after she convinced Teddy to take her to 401 Portage Street.

## CHAPTER SEVEN

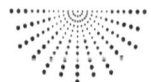

*A* few days had gone by since Becky had ruined her feet. As much as she'd wanted to get a look at 401 Portage Street, she had been forced to wait. The blisters on her heels had been unforgiving in any pair of shoes. There was no use trying to walk, let alone dance, in any pair she owned, so she'd lived like Teeter, in bare feet, and felt surprisingly liberated by it.

That morning when she woke up, she found Fanny bustling back and forth in the hallway outside her bedroom.

"What are you doing?" Becky asked.

"Oh, nothing. I just had such a wonderful evening that I felt like getting up early and taking care of a few things for your mother," Fanny said.

"Fine." Becky wrapped her robe around her before tying it tightly and was about to go downstairs when Fanny stopped her with one simple sentence.

"Adam White really is a fine dancer."

Becky knew she was being goaded. She knew Fanny lived for conflict and drama, and any response other than a shrug of the shoulders would be feeding right into her plan. But she couldn't help it. She squinted at Fanny.

"My Adam White?"

"Oh, come now, Rebecca. He isn't *yours*. You can't expect him to be a wallflower just because you don't show up. But don't you worry, I told him about your feet and how you'd been out with Stephen." Fanny grinned.

"Out with Stephen?" Becky remembered that when Stephen had fibbed for her, telling Kitty and Judge it was his fault she had hurt her feet, Fanny had not been in the room. "How do you know about that?"

"Your mama told me," Fanny stuttered.

"No she didn't," Becky snarled.

"What does it matter?" Fanny replied, standing her ground. "It's the truth, isn't it? I just passed it along to Adam when he asked where you were. I wouldn't worry if I were you. We had a wonderful time. And he was nothing but a gentleman when he drove me home."

"You were eavesdropping. What other things have you snooped around and overheard? I'll be sure to tell Mama when she gets back."

"Go on. I'm sure she'd be interested to know how you slipped into Stephen's room the night he stayed here on account of he had too much to drink. That will go over really swell."

With that, Fanny shrugged and walked into her room, shutting the door behind her. Becky knew better than to say anything else. In fact, she was quite proud of herself for not kicking in the door, dragging Fanny out by her lush, blond locks, and pummeling her until she begged for mercy. Instead, she took a deep breath, went downstairs, and poured herself a cup of coffee.

Her father, already seated at the table, watched her from behind his paper. "Good morning, sweetheart," he said suspiciously.

"Morning, Daddy," Becky said absently.

"Something the matter?"

"I don't know." She wanted to say something, but part of her didn't want anyone in the house to think there was a problem between her and Adam. She'd gone through so much trouble getting his foot in the door that if she were to complain that he had been a gentleman to Fanny, it would provide fodder for them to dislike him again. Not that she was sure they really did like him. They certainly liked Stephen. His blond hair and Southern drawl were enough to melt an iceberg in Antarctica. She did not want their simple kiss, which had meant nothing, to become a topic of conversation.

"Are you missing Mama?" Judge asked.

"Yeah. I think so." Becky did miss her mother. Strange how at this moment, she really realized that Kitty was gone and wished old Aunt Hortense would meet St. Peter soon so she could come back. It wasn't a very Christian thing to pray for, but she didn't want the old biddy to suffer. A swift death was sometimes the kindest thing that can happen to a person.

"Well, we got a telegram this morning. Seems Aunt Hortense is not doing well. Your Mama should be home within the week." He smiled, his eyes crinkling at the corners.

"Good. It's too quiet around here without her," Becky muttered.

"Would you like me to schedule some suitors to come visit so you don't get lonely?" he teased.

"Heavens no, Daddy."

"Are you sure? I think I saw a young man at the butcher shop who looked like he might be eligible. I know for a fact Hershel Sheel, the man who digs the plots in the cemetery, is single. I'm sure he'd be thrilled to make your acquaintance." Becky started to laugh. "I'm sure the postman knows of some boy with a questionable background who isn't choosy who might be interested in meeting you over some lemonade."

By this time, Becky had let go of her anger toward Fanny and was happy to say her mother's matchmaking was not missed. She shook her head as she laughed at her father, who sat across the table from her, straight-faced and serious as he manufactured a plethora of bachelors in the Savannah area.

"Daddy, that's too much." She coughed and took a sip of coffee. "You do know that I am partial to Mr. Adam White, don't you?"

"I had that feeling," Judge replied.

"And what do you think of him? I mean, really think of him?" Becky asked, hoping that Fanny had stayed in her room.

"I think he's a fine young man. I think of all the

fellas your mother has brought into this house who have eaten our food and drunk more lemonade than a man ever should, it was you who brought in the most promising," he said, but he raised his finger.

"But?" Becky leaned forward.

"But I don't like considering that there may be a man in my daughter's life who might... outrank me." Judge winked.

"Oh, Daddy. You know there ain't no boy who could do that. Not even Adam White. He comes close, but no cigar." Becky winked back. "Now, before we get too mushy, I was wondering what your plans were today. Mama will want a full account of what we've done while she was gone."

Judge was going to tend the tobacco fields as usual. Although he joked that he'd be eating his dinner in bed, an absolute no-no when Kitty was home. It was obvious he missed her. He did not seem interested in what Becky had planned for the evening, and that was a relief to her.

He headed off to find Clemont, the foreman of the fields. Clemont had been with the Mackenzies for several years and had become one of Judge's most faithful confidants. Becky was sure they enjoyed working the land together like other men enjoyed a mint julep together.

While he was out and Fanny was in her room, Becky casually strolled across the Mackenzie property to the Rockdale property next door. Teddy was there, bare-chested while hunched over his father's truck, working on the engine.

"My goodness. Is that Theodore Rockdale working with his hands? I'm suddenly struck with the vapors." Becky laid her wrist over her forehead and pretended to stagger.

"Well, look who's back on her feet." Teddy smiled. "How are you feeling, darling?"

"Much better, thank you. I'm ready to go dancing tonight. Are you game?" Becky asked.

"Of course. I'll call Martha."

"That's fine. Have we ever been to a joint on Portage Street?" she asked innocently.

"Portage? Not that I remember. Why?" Teddy asked.

"I got a tip from a canary that there is a joint at 401 Portage Street that's supposed to be the bee's knees. It's a ritzy part of town. You think we'll fit in?" Becky asked. She felt a little bad not telling her dear friend how she had come to know of this place, but part of her thought the less any of them knew, the better.

"Ritzy? Us? Fit in? Why darling, there isn't a place

in all Savannah that doesn't improve when we arrive," Teddy said, winking.

"Great. I'll be ready when you pull up." Becky turned to head back home.

"Is Fanny coming?" Teddy called after her.

Becky stopped, turned, and walked back to Teddy. "I'm sure she will," Becky said reluctantly. "She said that Adam danced with her and brought her home last night."

"That is true," Teddy replied.

"You'd tell me if I had something to worry about, wouldn't you?" Becky searched Teddy's face for some reassurance that she was worrying over nothing.

"Becky, you have more class in your pinky than Fanny has in her whole body. If Adam can't see that, he isn't worth the trouble." He smiled. "But hey, if this place is as shnazzy as you say, put on your best duds, add a little more lipstick, and show the palooka he's not the only fish in the pond. Sometimes a guy needs a good dose of jealousy to remind him of what he's got."

"You're my favorite egg, Teddy." Becky stood on tiptoe to give him a peck on the cheek. "See you tonight."

Becky took Teddy's advice and put on her

favorite black dress, which plunged rather daringly in the front and back and sparkled with little black sequins around every curve. When Becky saw the look on Fanny's face, she knew she was wearing the cat's pajamas.

"I've never seen that outfit on you, Rebecca," Fanny said as they went downstairs. "Are you sure your mother would approve of you wearing something so risqué?"

"Risqué? I'll have you know Mama picked this dress out for me when I was going stag to a New Year's Eve party two years ago. Needless to say, I wasn't alone at midnight," Becky replied as she hopped down the stairs. Her feet still stung a little in the toes, but she was not going to spend another night at home.

Teddy had already picked up Martha, and there was a very handsome Adam White sitting in the rumble seat. For a second, Becky fretted that he was there to pick up Fanny. Fanny certainly didn't mind flirting with him as soon as she saw him.

"Why, you do look dapper tonight, Mr. White," Fanny said. "I don't think any of the gentlemen in all of Paris looked as handsome as you do."

"Thank you, Fanny." He hopped out of the rumble seat and held the car door open for Fanny to scoot into the back seat. Then he turned his attention to Becky. "Feeling better?"

"Yes. Didn't you hear? I went running through a briar patch in my bare feet?" she joked.

"I wish you would have let me know. I would have carried you wherever you needed to go." He winked as she got closer to the car.

"Oh, come on, you two. This ain't no movie theater. Quit with the lovey-dovey, and let's make tracks. Becky, you look smashing!" Martha chirped from the front seat. "Sitting up front?"

"No. I'll sit in back and make sure Adam doesn't fall out along the way." She shimmied into the back seat before Adam shut the door. "Don't worry, darling. If you fall out, I'll make sure to make note of the street marker, and we'll pick you up on the way home."

The entire way, the group laughed, talked, and passed around a small flask of hooch that made Becky think of the one she had safely tucked away in her room. By the time they got to 401 Portage, everyone was feeling warm all over. The sound of music could be heard from the street, but they weren't certain where it was coming from.

"There we are. 401 Portage." Martha pointed to a dark-green awning. "It's a furniture store. Great.

How did they know I was looking for a teak armoire?"

Adam held the door open, and everyone filed in. The store owner, a tough-looking guy with a thick mustache and eyebrows to match, looked them up and down. Teddy did the talking since he was the slickest in the group, and before they knew it—and after he slipped the man a five-dollar bill—they were walking through the back of the store and down a long corridor that connected to the building next door.

"Wow! This is a sight!" Martha said as they walked into the speakeasy.

The walls were painted red. The sconces on the walls gave everything a soft, warm glow. The bar was a mile long, the band was four cats who could really jam, and the dance floor was packed. Teddy found an empty table while Adam grabbed Becky's hand and pulled her to the dance floor.

"I've been waiting days for this," he said before he kissed her on the lips.

"I was hoping to hear that. Fanny told me you were just the most divine dancer and a real gentleman when you drove her home." Becky watched Adam's face as he smirked.

"She didn't tell you that Martha had too much to

drink, so Teddy took her home, and she had no other way of getting back?"

"No. She left out that little detail."

Becky felt silly. She should have known by now that nothing Fanny said was ever the straight dope. The girl lived on drama and conflict, and Becky played into her hands every time. Right now, she saw her cousin at the bar with a fella at her side, already offering to buy her a drink. She was probably telling him how they did it in Paris.

"Is that why you are dressed the way you are?" Adam asked as he held her close and swung her around the dance floor.

"What's wrong with how I'm dressed? I thought I looked nice," Becky said.

"Nice isn't the word." Adam leaned down to her ear.

He smelled good, like oranges and newspaper ink. He was wearing a white shirt open at the collar. His trousers hung perfectly on his hips, and his boots weren't polished but looked rugged even as he glided across the dance floor.

"I'm getting some ideas in my head that maybe I shouldn't," he teased.

"Oh really?" Becky giggled and squeezed him closer.

Just then, she felt a tap on her shoulder. Her body tensed, and she was sure she'd turn around to see the angry face of Leonard Brennan staring down at her. She'd completely lost her head with Adam there. How could she be so stupid?

"Mind if I cut in?" Stephen Penbroke asked.

"Stephen. What a surprise," Becky said.

Adam reached out his hand to shake. "Be my guest, Steve. I'll get us a couple of drinks," Adam said, giving Becky a peck on the cheek and then strolling off toward the bar.

Stephen quickly took his place. "And to think I almost said I wasn't going to come when Fanny invited me." He looked down at Becky's dress, making her blush like mad. "I'd have kicked myself for days if I missed this view."

"You stop that. Don't be a cad," she huffed. "So Fanny invited you."

"Are you sorry she did?"

"Of course not, Stephen. I think you and Fanny make a lovely couple. In fact, she's probably wondering why you haven't danced with her yet."

Becky looked out into the crowd and saw a familiar face. It wasn't Leonard Brennan's angry face. It was Violet, and she was frantically waving. It looked like she was shouting too. Becky looked at her and then back at Stephen, who was blathering on about something; she wasn't sure what.

"You and I are cut from the same cloth, Becky. You've got to know that," Stephen said.

"I'm sorry. This is all a little confusing." She wasn't lying. "I need to find the ladies' room. If you'll excuse me."

Without worrying about Stephen, Becky hurried across the room, sliding and gliding through the other dancers and patrons. Stephen was probably annoyed with her for leaving him so abruptly. More than one fella gave her a wink and a nod as she passed. If her dress hadn't worked on Adam, it certainly worked on just about every other fella in the place.

Farther back into the club, Becky saw shady characters in high-backed booths with little table candles casting shadows over their faces. As she watched out of the corner of her eye, she didn't see anyone who resembled Leonard. But there were quite a few big fellows who had beautiful ladies hanging off their arms—ladies with a little too much powder on their faces who smoked cigarettes from long black filters and had loads and loads of ice hanging from their wrists, necks, and ears. Waiters in tuxedos quickly replaced empty bottles of champagne with full ones in silver buckets. Long-legged girls with tight finger waves in their hair strolled through the crowd, offering cigars, cigarettes, chewing gum, and Hershey's chocolate from big boxes braced at their waists.

Violet was walking to the back of the building. Unlike at the last place Becky had seen her, there wasn't a long hallway in the back of the speakeasy but a creepy and dimly lit flight of stairs that led down. Becky saw Violet at the very bottom, walking as if she knew the route well.

Becky looked over her shoulder and saw no one following her. In fact, no one was even paying any attention to her. Quickly, she went down the stairs. To her right was a room where a quiet, serious poker game was taking place. Across from it was another room lined with chaise lounge chairs and plump loveseats on which several people were lolling about. It didn't take long for Becky to realize they were smoking opium. Their eyes were ringed red, and they didn't notice her at all.

In still another room, Becky saw a man with two women in various states of dress. Why was Violet leading her down here? Sure, she knew that not all speakeasies were alike, and some catered to a more deviant clientele, but this was more than she had bargained for. Still, she followed Violet, who stopped before a door and looked directly at her before stepping inside. Becky winced, already sure whatever was in the room was going to be disturbing. She had no idea how disturbing.

CHAPTER EIGHT

The room was in the middle of the hallway. Becky didn't dare go snooping to see what was going on in the other rooms. With shoulders squared and her chin high, she strolled confidently into the room as if she belonged there, prepared to confront anyone or anything. But the room was empty. With the exception of a small couch, the room was just four walls, a floor, and a ceiling.

Becky swallowed hard. Just as she was about to turn around and leave, Violet slowly began to appear out of thin air. She didn't see Becky. She was talking with someone who wasn't there. At first she was happy. She was smiling and reached out as if she was about to hug someone. But her arms were pushed to her sides by invisible hands.

"What's wrong?" Violet asked, even though no words came out. She was talking to someone who was mad at her. She shook her head. "It's safe. I hid it."

Becky could almost hear her speaking, but she knew there was no sound coming from the film playing out in front of her. This was a flashback to something that had happened to Violet. Becky wanted to run back to her group, toss back a good stiff drink, and leave, never to cross the threshold of 401 Portage Street again. But it was too late. She couldn't leave Violet. Not like this. Not replaying this miserable experience.

Becky continued to watch as Violet put her hands out in front of her. Her lips were moving so fast that Becky couldn't make out what Violet was saying. Her shoulders were pulled up around her ears, her hands extended as she tried to explain something. Violet backed up until she was against the wall. Her body jumped as if she had been startled by a loud noise. A shout! She shook her head.

And that was when it came out of nowhere: a slap so hard that it knocked Violet's head into the wall. She put her hand to her cheek and started crying. But that didn't matter to whoever was hitting her. And they didn't stop there. Violet put up her hands in a feeble attempt to defend herself. Her arm was slapped aside. She was grabbed by her beautiful long black hair and dragged to the couch.

Standing stone still, Becky watched as Violet was beaten. Even though his image wasn't there, Becky knew the man who had killed Violet was doing this to her. Her poor spirit had to wander these depraved halls and repeatedly relive this beating in death.

Leonard Brennan had done this to her. And if he'd done this to Violet and still had the nerve to claim he loved her, what would he do to Becky if he caught up with her?

Over and over, Violet was hit until she collapsed on the floor. Becky's eyes were filled with tears. Her heart broke for the girl. What was she going to do?

"Hey, honey. You here for me?"

Becky whirled around to see a big Bruno standing there. He was a handsome man, but there was an oily, greasy tinge to him. His eyes were red with alcohol and maybe opium. His suit was expensive, but there were stains on it, and his shoes weren't shined.

"Don't cry, doll. I'll take care of him for you. Just

point the louse out for me, and his mama will be reading about him in the papers tomorrow," the man said with spit in the corners of his mouth.

"Mr. Elby Ferris, she's not for you," said an older woman with long black lashes circling her eyes and liver spots on the thin hand that raised a cigarette to her mouth. "Here comes yours."

She pointed to a woman in a red dress and black stockings, who looked tired even as she smiled.

"That's too bad. If you ever want to earn a little extra scratch, come and talk to my associate here, Miss Chantilly," Mr. Ferris said. "I'm willing to pay double." He looked Becky up and down, making her wish she was wearing her father's baggy plowing dungarees and work shirt. But with Mr. Ferris, she was sure it probably wouldn't matter.

Before Becky could step out of the room, Mr. Ferris grabbed the girl in the red dress and yanked her to him, covering her face with sloppy kisses. Miss Chantilly grabbed Becky's hand in a viselike grip and tugged her out of the room.

"You lookin' for me, honey?" She looked out from heavy eyelids coated with liner and mascara.

"I don't think so." Becky sniffled, pulling her arm away before she wiped her eyes.

"You're not looking for work?"

"Work?"

"Oh, that's what we sometimes call it," Miss Chantilly said coldly. "Look, don't waste my time, or I'll have Officer Ferris arrest you for loitering once he's finished."

"Officer?" Becky stuttered.

"Look, honey, if you aren't running rum or looking for work, you got no business being down here," Miss Chantilly grumbled.

"Did you know Violet Darcy?" Becky didn't want to ask this question. What was she doing? She wanted to climb out of this swamp and go back to her friends and forget all about it. But the words just tumbled out, as they had a habit of doing.

Miss Chantilly grabbed her arm again and squeezed. She was incredibly strong for a woman who looked to be around sixty years old and probably hadn't seen sunlight in months if not longer.

"You won't ever mention that name again if you know what's good for you." Miss Chantilly looked at the room in which they'd left Officer Ferris and the girl in the red dress. "Take my advice, kid. Leave and don't come back." She gave Becky a shove before turning her back and disappearing into a room at the end of the hallway.

Becky thought of following her, but the sounds coming from the room she had just seen Violet beaten in made her turn and run.

She couldn't help it. Tears began to flow freely down her cheeks. What was happening? What kind of place was this? Why had Violet let herself be treated this way? She had been kind and sweet. Why hadn't she asked for help or run away?

Becky pounded up the stairs, making sure to keep her eyes focused straight ahead of her so as not to see what else might have been happening in the rooms. She wanted to go to Willie's, where she knew almost everyone and there weren't any sleazy Officer Ferrises or Miss Chantillys. Some people might say this was real life, that Becky had been so sheltered growing up on the tobacco plantation that she didn't know the seedier side of life existed. That wasn't true. She knew it did. She just didn't expect to see it play out in front of her with a person she knew starring in it as the corpse.

When she finally made it back to the table, she grabbed a glass, not knowing whose it was or what was in it, and tossed it back. It didn't help her nerves. Her body trembled, and she still had tears in her eyes.

Adam was smiling when he looked up to see her, but his face fell, and he was on his feet in an instant. "Becky, what's wrong?" Adam asked.

"Would you get me home?" She swallowed hard.

"What happened? I left you for just a few minutes, and..." Just then, Stephen came sauntering up, looking annoyed. "What did you do to her?"

"What are you talking about?" Stephen replied.

"Becky, did he do something to you?" Adam asked.

"No. I just want to leave. Please, Adam, get me home," Becky pleaded, her eyes getting redder by the minute.

"I'll take you home, Becky," Stephen offered.

"Over my dead body," Adam barked. "Don't think I haven't noticed how you've been looking at her since you got here. And I don't mean to this place. I mean since you got to town."

"Oh yeah? How am I looking at her?" Stephen was about four inches shorter than Adam but stood right up to him. "Maybe I'm looking at her the way she wishes you would."

"What's going on?" Martha interrupted.

"Hey, fellas." Teddy stepped in. "Come on. We're all friends here. Let's not make a scene. They'll kick us out one at a time like a group of hobos. Come on. Drinks on me."

"You don't have any idea what you're talking about." Adam took a step closer to Stephen, who didn't back up.

Becky grabbed Adam by his arm and yanked hard to get his attention. "Stephen didn't do anything, Adam. It's not him. Please, would you take me home?" Becky pleaded. She wasn't sure if Adam even heard her. He was too busy staring at Stephen, who was also oblivious to her presence. "Teddy?" She looked to her longtime friend for help.

"All right, fellas. Enough is enough. Let's go." He stepped between Adam and Stephen, snapping them out of their rage and calming things down for the moment. "Come on. Let's blow this pop stand. The frog water is a little too pricey for my blood anyway."

"Becky, are you all right?" Martha asked. "You look like you just saw a ghost."

"Ha, that's funny." Becky chuckled. "I saw something. I saw more than I bargained for. You wouldn't believe it if I told you. I saw…"

"Saw what, honey?" Martha asked as she grabbed her purse.

But Becky didn't answer. Across the room, standing no fewer than thirty feet from her, was Leonard Brennan. He was staring right at her.

"Martha, we're in trouble."

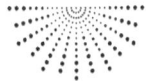

# CHAPTER NINE

*T*he band jumped into a rendition of "Ain't Nobody's Business If I Do," and within seconds, everyone was on their feet and on the dance floor. Becky grabbed Martha's hand.

"I don't have time to explain!" she shouted above the music and crowd. "But we have to get out of here!"

"Becky? What's going on?" Adam shouted.

"We need to leave!" Becky said on tiptoes into Adam's ear.

"What for?" he argued.

Becky scanned the room and saw Leonard Brennan trying to maneuver his way to their table through the crowd. He was glaring at her.

"Because if we don't, that guy is going to fit me

for a Chicago raincoat!" Becky said as she pointed to Leonard.

Anyone who went to any speakeasy in Savannah had seen Leonard Brennan at one time or another. He was impossible to miss. Plus, having Violet hanging off his arm had been like having a spotlight focused on him. But now he didn't have Violet and was just a big gorilla of a man on a mission to pound Becky into the ground along with anyone else who got in his way.

"What do you say we blow this pop stand?" Teddy asked, oblivious to the danger they were in. Martha grabbed his hand and he grabbed Fanny, who in turn took hold of Stephen's arm as he was getting ready to say something to Adam again.

"Where are we going?" he asked Martha.

"We gotta get out of here!" she shouted in his face over the music and pointed to Leonard Brennan.

"What did you do?" He looked down at Martha.

"Not me! Becky!" she yelled.

"I should have known," he replied. "Okay! Follow me!"

Linked together like children on a playground, Teddy pulled everyone toward the entrance where they'd first come in. But a big Bruno was standing there, obviously a friend of Leonard's, who pointed out the group to the bouncer sitting there.

"Nope. Back this train up," Teddy said, quickly yanking Martha back toward the dance floor. He skirted the edge of the dancing crowd, keeping the revelers in between them and Leonard, until they reached another corridor that looked like it led to an exit. But it was crowded with fellas moving crates of booze in and out. There was no getting past them.

"Another dead end," Teddy huffed.

"Don't say *dead*," Martha quipped.

"This is a nightmare," Becky huffed. "It's all my fault."

"Becky, what the heck is going on?" Adam huffed and squeezed her hand.

"I'll tell you everything, but first, we have to get out of here."

"My shoes are killing me," Fanny said as she shuffled along, holding tightly to Stephen's arm. "I didn't expect to be running the Boston Marathon."

"This isn't how I expected things to turn out, Fanny," Stephen said, squeezing her hand and clenching his teeth as they pulled each other along.

"Now isn't the time to talk about this," Fanny replied.

"No. It isn't. But you and I need to have a serious

talk." Stephen looked at Fanny, making her almost lose her balance as they were pulled through people.

"That way!" Teddy pointed to the stairs Becky had just come up.

She stopped on a dime, squeezing Martha's hand. "Not that way." She stared and shook her head.

"I think it's the only way," Martha said. "Becky, we have to get out of here. I think the ranks are closing in."

Becky looked around and saw Leonard in one direction and another fella just as big coming from the opposite direction. She didn't want to go back down those stairs. The vision of Violet being manhandled squeezed her heart beneath her ribs. The people down there who could have helped, could have stepped in had they not been engaged in their own depraved behavior, were still down there.

"Come on!" Adam shouted. "Teddy, lead the way!"

The music was pounding in Becky's ears. Then, as if someone had shut a heavy door, all she heard was their footsteps, Fanny complaining about her feet, Stephen yelling for Teddy to hurry, Martha calling Becky but sounding like she was a million miles away. Becky focused, squinting, just as *Officer* Elby Ferris stepped out of the room she'd seen Violet in. The girl in the red dress hurried out and in the direction of Miss Chantilly, who stood at the end of the hallway with her hands on her hips. Miss Chantilly seemed to show no concern for the girl and instead was glaring at the group traipsing down the hallway making a ruckus.

"Well, back so soon?" Elby smirked at Becky, smoothing his naturally wavy blond hair away from his face. "Come talk to me, sweetheart. Let me buy you a drink."

"What are you doing down here?" Miss Chantilly snapped.

"Nothing. Just passing through." Teddy winked, pulling the group along with him toward a door that had to be an exit.

"What's the rush, doll?" Elby was as big as Adam and looked him up and down as if sizing up the competition. He didn't seem intimidated.

Just then, behind them at the other end of the hallway, Leonard appeared with two of his associates behind him.

"We're leaving," Adam said, stepping between Elby and Becky.

"Oh, I hope it isn't on account of that piece of garbage." Elby jerked his thumb in Leonard's direction. "You can stay. He's nobody."

"Becky, how do you know this guy?" Martha

whispered, but Becky's head was starting to swim. She looked behind him into the empty room and was sure she saw a blurry image of Violet standing there. The vision made her squint and blink until finally it came into focus. Poor Violet's bloody, beaten face screamed. Becky heard no words but saw what she was saying. She was screaming RUN.

Looking behind her with wild eyes, Becky saw Leonard and began to tremble.

"Step aside, Ferris. This doesn't concern you," Leonard said through clenched teeth.

"Or else what, tough guy?" Officer Elby Ferris licked his lips, his red eyes aiming at Leonard. "You gonna try and stop me?"

Becky didn't know what Elby Ferris needed to be stopped from doing, but she couldn't take it anymore. With Martha's hand still in hers, Becky grabbed Adam by the arm and yanked him toward Miss Chantilly and the only way out of this place. Fanny and Stephen followed close behind.

"Just wait a minute!" Miss Chantilly tried to stop them, but Teddy, normally always the gentleman, pushed her aside and darted to the door. With every muscle, he pushed the door open, revealing another set of stairs barely lit by an overhead light. But these concrete steps led up, and Becky could smell the fresh air. The entire group passed Teddy as he held the door open, shouting and waving his arms.

Martha and Becky still held hands. Adam had let go and stood inside the door to make sure the girls and Stephen got out. Once they were all outside the building, he grabbed the door and yanked it shut.

"Where's your car?" Teddy asked Stephen.

"Around the corner," he replied as they continued to run away from 401 Portage Street.

"Becky, are you all right?" Martha asked. "Becky?"

Before Becky could say anything, she was consumed by darkness. Her body shut down in the middle of an alley—just like Violet's had after a bullet had been put in her head.

# CHAPTER TEN

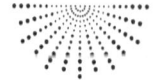

"*S*he's coming around."

Becky could hear a female voice. It wasn't Martha, and it certainly wasn't Fanny. Oh no. Could it be Violet? Was she dead? Had she passed over into the realm of spirits?

"She looks awful," another scratchy female voice replied.

"Hey," Becky replied weakly, fluttering her eyes open. The first thing she saw was Ophelia's wrinkled face. "*I* look awful?"

"Ha. She's all right." Ophelia smirked and patted Becky's head.

"How many times have you come to my place only to faint on my sofa?" Madame Cecelia asked.

She was wearing her usual gypsy-type dress of a bright colored pattern and a scarf in her hair.

"I think I fainted before I got here. How did I…" As Becky opened her eyes wider, she saw Stephen's head hovering over hers, upside down.

"How are you feeling?" he asked.

"Like I drank too much. And I barely had a drop. Where is the rest of the gang? Where's Adam?" she asked, pushing herself up on her elbows.

"Oh, uh, I told them to meet us here. I didn't know where else to go, and I thought it better if we split up. I didn't think going back to the plantation was a good idea, since I had no idea if we were being followed," Stephen said while shrugging. "There are a lot of things I don't know."

"You've got that right, brother," Ophelia replied, sizing him up.

"Mother, is anyone minding the store? We could be getting robbed blind down there." Madame Cecelia put her hand on her hip. "We are still open for another hour."

"Call me if you need me," Ophelia replied as she opened the front door to the apartment and stepped out onto the stair landing before pulling the door shut behind her.

"Do you want to tell me what happened?" Cecelia asked.

"We had a run-in with a real bad crowd," Stephen said as Becky swung her feet to the floor and felt over her finger waves, patting them into place the same way her mother would do.

"I see." Cecelia looked Stephen up and down. "I've got some tea that will perk you right up. Just a little arrowroot, some ginger, maybe some wart of toad."

"Sounds swell," Becky said.

"You know, you could just come and visit me for the heck of it. There doesn't always need to be an emergency or someone chasing you. The last time that happened, I needed a new window." Cecelia smiled.

"I didn't know we were coming here," Becky said. "I'm so sorry. I hope we haven't brought trouble right up to your doorstep again. If anything happens, you simply must tell me immediately so I can arrange for my daddy to reimburse you. It's the least I could do for everything you've done for me."

"Don't mention it. So, you were being chased?" Cecelia asked as the water in the kettle boiled. "You've got some of his mojo on you. He's a bad man."

"I think he killed his girlfriend. She was just as

sweet as any Georgia peach, and she was found dead in the alley outside her apartment," Becky replied.

"Is that the girl I read about in the papers? She was named after some kind of flower?" Cecelia asked.

"Yes. Her name was Violet Darcy. She was dating this big goon, and she did something to make him madder than usual. We often saw her with a couple love taps, if you catch my meaning," Becky replied, shaking her head.

Cecelia gave her the cup of tea and offered one to Stephen, who declined.

"And you knew this woman?" Cecelia asked.

"I knew her from around the clubs. She treated everyone like they were her friends. Usually, a girl who looks like Violet did thinks she's the Queen of Sheba. But not Violet. She was just... just a good person who didn't deserve to be murdered. Especially by that monster, Leonard Brennan." Becky winced as if saying his name was painful.

"How do you know it was him?" Cecelia asked.

Becky told her she had all but heard him confess. But she knew she couldn't go to the police with just what she had overheard.

"What you heard, Becky, is vague at best. It sounds like an admission. It also sounds like he quit dating her or he quit buying her jewelry. It could be a hundred different things, and that is what Leonard Brennan would say if you asked him." Cecelia cleared her throat. "If he doesn't bust you in the chops first."

"But he knows I heard him. He knows I was at Violet's apartment." Becky winced again as if the words hurt as she confessed them.

"You were at her apartment?" Stephen asked. "When?"

"The day you picked me up and gave me a ride home. The day my mother was leaving for Aunt Hortense's house," Becky said.

"You were running from Leonard Brennan? He saw you? Becky, do you know how crazy that was? Do you know how dangerous he is? He's a killer."

"I know that, Stephen. Do you really think I don't know that?" Becky rolled her eyes as she took a sip of tea.

"What are you going to do?" Stephen huffed. "I want you to know, whatever it is I'll help you. No matter what."

"That's very chivalrous of you, Stephen, but I'm sure it won't come to anything. Not if I can get to the police before he fills me full of daylight." Becky sighed. "This tea is delicious."

"It's the spider webs and bat wings that give it its flavor." Cecelia winked. "Come over here and sit down. Let's see what the cards have to say."

Becky set her cup down on the dainty side table next to the couch and slowly stood up, rubbing the back of her head. There wasn't a goose egg back there, but it was tender where she'd apparently hit the sidewalk with her noggin. She took a seat, and Stephen paced the floor.

"You are seriously going to do this now?" he squawked.

"Stephen, Madame Cecelia has helped me in more ways than I care to admit. Now, if you don't like this sort of thing, that's fine. I don't believe she asked to read your cards. Now you can either pipe down or be on your merry way. I'll find a way home."

"You don't really think I'd let you out of my sight after what happened tonight?" Stephen asked. "I think… we should go to the police, and the sooner the better."

Madame Cecelia looked Stephen up and down as she shuffled her deck of tarot cards.

"Cut the deck for me," she instructed Becky, who blinked and admitted to feeling better. Madame Cecelia shuffled the cards once more and then began to lay them out in a pattern in front of her. In the center was the card labelled "Death." As soon as Stephen saw it, peeking over Becky's shoulder, he erupted in a fit of anger.

"What the heck is that? You see, Becky! This is not good! We shouldn't be wasting any more time here. We need to talk to the police!" Stephen shouted as he continued his pacing.

"The death card does not mean death the way you see it, Stephen," Madame Cecelia cooed. "It means something will be changing."

"Stephen, if this is too nerve-racking for you, I'll kindly ask that you take a seat over there." Becky pointed to the sofa.

Stephen shook his head and paced to the far end of the room, where he studied some knickknacks on a shelf.

"I see the initials A.W."

"That's Adam. Adam White." Becky gulped. "Is he all right?"

"There is a change between you and him."

Suddenly Stephen's ears perked up. He pretended not to listen but cocked his head in their direction.

"Is it bad?" Becky asked, all thoughts of dying at the hands of Leonard Brennan had left her head.

"I can't tell. There is something in the way. A

shadow. Fog. I can't tell. I also see a uniform. Police. Something gets resolved. This is a regular logjam, Becky. There is so much going on that it's all over-lapping and fading and resurfacing. I can't make heads or tails out of it." Madame Cecelia shook her head. "But a strange ally is going to emerge. Be on the lookout. That's the only thing I can see for sure, and the only thing I can tell is it's a man."

"What do you do when you get a reading like that?" Becky asked.

"I usually let a few days pass and try again." She winked. "In the meantime, finish your tea, and then you'd best be on your way. If I didn't hear the sound of breaking glass downstairs, I'd say it was a safe bet no one followed you here."

"Sorry, Cecelia, but that didn't really help. In fact, I think it made things worse." Becky chuckled. "Stephen, didn't you say you told Teddy to meet us here?" Becky asked. "They should have been here by now. Unless something happened to them."

"Um, well, I assumed they'd meet us here." He cleared his throat and tugged at his cuffs beneath his jacket. "I'll go check and see if they are waiting downstairs." With that, he opened the front door and stepped out of the apartment.

"I wonder what's eating him?" Becky mused.

"Thanks for your help and the tea. I promise that next time, I'll come and visit for no reason."

"Count Ernesto and I will be featured at a party for the mayor's birthday," Madame Cecelia said. "We are part of the entertainment. It isn't for a month or so, but perhaps you can find a way to attend. I'm sure the daughter of a prominent tobacco farmer could find her way onto the guest list."

"That sounds ducky. I might even forego the guest list and crash the shindig just for kicks." Becky bounced her shoulders. "Give me the details the next time we visit."

"Becky, Stephen is hiding something. He has feelings for you, but his motive is questionable. Tread lightly."

"Oh, I know. Stephen thinks that we share some kind of intimate bond." She thought of their kiss and wasn't too displeased to recall it. But it wasn't what was on her mind. In fact, the truth was that a kiss from Stephen was the last thing on her mind after all that had happened tonight. She wanted to see Adam more than anything. "He's just a little bit of a playboy. I can handle him."

With that, Becky left Madame Cecelia and went downstairs. Before she even got to the first floor she could hear Stephen arguing with Ophelia. What possessed him to do such a thing to the woman? What could have started this?

"You're not telling the truth," Ophelia said.

"I don't know what you are talking about, but you need to mind your own business. None of this concerns you," Stephen snapped.

"That girl comes here for help. She has a gift. You will never understand," Ophelia said. "And you have a bad smell around you."

"What is going on?" Becky asked as she looked around the store. There was just one older man perusing the strange roots in bins on the southern side of the store.

"Nothing. Are you done with all of this? Can we go now?" Stephen asked.

"What about Teddy and Martha and Adam? Were they here?"

"No." Stephen cleared his throat. "Come on. Let's get going. I'll take you home."

"Bye, Ophelia." Becky waved.

"You'll have a bad smell too." Ophelia replied, making Becky wince and squint at her before she walked out the door.

"What is she talking about? Why were you arguing with her? She's a harmless old woman. Well, she's an old woman."

Becky scanned the sidewalk. There were lots of people still out and about. The air was warm, and the smell of car exhaust hovered along the street, making her wish she'd never gone to 401 Portage Street. It was a perfect night for dancing, and it was blown already.

"She said I smelled."

"That riled you up so much you had to yell at her? If that's all it took, you wouldn't believe what she's said to me since I met her." Becky chuckled. "Where is everyone? Teddy should have gotten here by now, don't you think?"

Stephen didn't answer but instead paced back and forth on the sidewalk in front of his car.

"Stephen? You said you told them to meet us here. Aren't you worried?"

"No. I brought you here because you wouldn't wake up." He cleared his throat. "I scooped you up in my arms before Adam could. If I'd have left you with him, who knows what might have happened? Trust me, Becky, the guy doesn't function well under pressure."

"What are you saying?"

"I'm saying that I said I'd take you for help and that the rest of them should go home." Stephen planted one foot then the other and put both hands on his waist. "Teddy is a swell guy, and he and Martha make a perfect couple. But neither one of them is going to amount to much without the help of their family's money. Fanny, well, she's got her sights set on a fella. If he were smart, he'd jump at it. It might be enough to pull him out of the low-level ranks he's in."

"You're talking about Adam, aren't you?" Becky asked.

"Becky, you and I are cut from the same cloth. We don't just love the South, we are rife with it in our veins. I understand you and your family in a way no Yankee ever will," Stephen said. "Perhaps I went about this all wrong. Maybe I should have been the gentleman and challenged that big oaf to a duel or something. But I didn't. Instead, I swooped in while he panicked, and I got you somewhere safe."

"And you left them? Do you know where they went? Do you know if they were followed?" Becky asked as she wrung her hands.

"I didn't leave them. I saw them pile into Teddy's car and speed off. If anything, they left you," Stephen said. "Once you were in my car, I hit the gas. I wasn't sure if we were being followed or not. A guy like Leonard Brennan knows people all over the place. Heavies, hobos, coppers, you name it, and he's got half of them on the take. I couldn't trust anyone. But I had to get you off the street. That's what I did."

"For that I am grateful," Becky said, lifting her chin. "I'd like to go home now."

Without saying a word, Stephen held the door open for Becky, and she scooted in. Within seconds, they were heading in the direction of the Mackenzie plantation. She couldn't wait to see it. It felt as if she'd been gone for days. When she arrived, she was shocked at what she saw. So was Stephen.

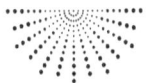

# CHAPTER ELEVEN

"We've been worried sick about you, gal!" Martha ran up to the car. Her mascara had smeared around her eyes. "You just collapsed on the street before any of us knew what was happening."

"Becky, you sure do know how to end an evening," Teddy said. "It would have been nice if you'd told us where you were going. But we're glad you made it home."

"Stephen took me to Madame Cecelia's store," Becky muttered and looked at Adam, who was on the porch with Fanny.

"I knew it." Martha snapped her fingers. "I should have thought of that. I was in such a panic. We didn't know if Leonard and his goons would be coming after us or what."

Becky looked to Adam. He shook Fanny off his arm and came charging toward Stephen, who was not shy about advancing.

"You've got a lot of nerve showing up here," Adam hissed.

"Sorry. I didn't think it would be prudent to let the lady just lie in the middle of the street," Stephen shot back. "That might be how you treat your women up north, but we do things differently in Georgia."

"Hold on, fellas. No one's been hurt. We all survived the night," Teddy said, trying to get between them. "Come on. I'll bet Mr. Mackenzie's got a bottle of something good. Let's crank up the Victrola, pour down a couple of glasses, and breathe easy for a while."

"I'll show you how we do things up north," Adam said, taking another step closer.

"Come on, Yankee. Let's see what you've got." Stephen brought his fists up just as Adam dove toward him.

Becky slipped in next to Teddy and desperately pushed against Adam's broad chest to get his attention.

"Stop! Stop all of this!" Becky yelled. But instead of getting through to either of them, she got shoved to the ground.

Martha ran to her side. Fanny stayed on the porch, watching the whole thing as if it was the Saturday-afternoon movie at the Bijou Theater in town.

Stephen swung at Adam. Adam swung at Stephen. Each guy got a lick in before Adam charged with so much force they both landed on the ground. With more rolling around and kicking up dust than actual damage being done, no one noticed when Judge Mackenzie came out of his front porch in his robe and pajamas. And his 12-gauge shotgun.

BOOM! Chah-chink! The spent shell clattered on the porch as Judge cocked the second shell into place.

Everyone froze. Becky let out a sigh of relief. If anyone could bring order to a situation, it was her father. She got up from the ground with Martha and dusted off her pretty black dress, which had been completely ruined by the night's events. Stephen and Adam had paused in the midst of their tussle to stare at her daddy.

"If you two gentlemen want to fight, take it off my land!" Judge scowled.

Adam was the first to get to his feet. He kicked Stephen's leg as he walked toward the porch. "I'm sorry, Mr. Mackenzie."

"I'm sorry, too, sir," Stephen said. "I wasn't thinking."

"How much have you boys had to drink tonight?" Judge asked.

"Not nearly enough," Teddy said, brushing off his fine striped shirt. "Seems our evening was cut short by a—"

Martha stepped on his toe.

"I wasn't feeling well, Uncle Judge," she lied for Becky. "We thought that maybe we could imbibe a gin or two here, closer to home. Just in case I felt light-headed again."

"Martha, that would be fine if you think you should. Perhaps Teddy should run you home." Judge looked at the group suspiciously.

"Daddy, Martha said she hadn't eaten all day. I think that is her problem. Mind if I scare up something in the kitchen so she can get her wits about her?" Becky took Adam by the hand and pulled him toward the porch.

"Go on. But don't disturb Moxley and Lucretia. They're done for the day and don't need the likes of any of you disturbing their sleep," Judge said. "Neither do I, for that matter. If you boys can't get along and you continue this display, you'll have a backside full of buckshot. Do not try me. Either of you."

"No sir, Mr. Mackenzie." Adam looked down at the ground, shamefaced.

"We won't, Mr. Mackenzie," Stephen added. They were like two boys who had gotten caught throwing a baseball through the window of a neighbor's house.

Judge nodded at the group and went back inside.

"Adam, would you be a dear and assist me in the kitchen? Teddy, you know where everything is at. Why don't you fix everyone something cold to drink?" Becky said as she dragged Adam past Fanny and into the house.

Once in the kitchen, she looked at him sternly. "Can I ask what just happened out there? My Lord, as if we all haven't been through enough tonight," Becky said as she pointed for several small plates to be brought down from a high shelf.

"Becky, there is something about Stephen Penbroke that rubs me the wrong way," Adam said as he carefully put the plates on the counter.

Becky went into the pantry and grabbed a bag of potato chips and dumped them into a pretty pale-green bowl. "It couldn't be that he was brought here by my mother for the sole purpose of marrying me off to him?" Becky replied as she grabbed some bread and the plate of butter from the icebox.

"Maybe that has something to do with it," Adam replied reluctantly.

"Don't you trust me?" Becky said as she angrily buttered the slices of bread then cut them into triangles.

"Of course, I trust you. I—"

"Because I think I've done a top-drawer job trusting you around Fanny. She's been circling around you like a vulture over a coyote carcass for I don't know how long now, and I haven't said boo about it," Becky said, her chest out and her eyes on the work at hand.

"You noticed that, too, huh?" Adam said.

"How could I not?" Becky replied then walked to the kitchen door and looked toward the sitting room, where Teddy was setting up the record player. "I've learned my lesson to look around corners in my own house. The walls have ears, and they are always attached to Fanny. That sounds rather crude, doesn't it?"

Adam chuckled. "I think your cousin and Mr. Penbroke have been communicating."

"Whatever do you mean?" Becky asked.

"Let's not worry about it now. I think we all need to discuss what happened tonight with Leonard Brennan. How are we ever going to show our faces at any respectable speakeasy again?" Adam shook his head.

"There are plenty of dives that'll take us just fine." Becky smiled then looked down at her plate of bread and butter and the bowl of potato chips.

She contemplated telling Adam what she'd seen. He knew about her special talent of seeing the dead. So far, he'd been just a peach about all of it. But this was different. This was dangerous, and everyone could have gotten really hurt. She decided not to tell him about what she had seen and done at Violet's apartment. She'd wait until it was really necessary.

Little did she know that there was someone else looking for the little treasures she'd collected.

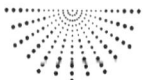

*a* few days had gone by, and Becky was climbing the walls. She hadn't gone out to any speakeasies and had had to relegate her dances to Teddy in the sitting room.

Kitty had sent word that Aunt Hortense's youngest son was coming to see Kitty with his wife.

"The one with the little monsters?" Becky asked Judge as they enjoyed an afternoon cocktail on the porch.

"That would be the one. They are trying to make good to get their inheritance." Judge chuckled. "That woman will take every penny with her, you mark my words."

"So, what have you got planned this evening, Daddy? I noticed that Lucretia has been cooking some really delicious desserts that have been suspiciously disappearing during the course of the night," Becky teased her father.

"Fanny's been eating them," he whispered.

Becky started to laugh. "I think you might be enjoying this time without Mama around. Maybe I should make an effort to get out of the house tonight so you can have it to yourself. You can smoke your cigars and listen to that crazy 'In the Good Old Summertime' as loud as you like it while Lucretia leaves the pecan pie she's making out for you to eat."

"I told you, it's Fanny," Judge whispered again. "But don't feel you have to leave on my account. Tonight might be a bit of a surprise. I thought I'd invite the Rockdale boys over, as well as a few of the gents from town, to join me in a game of poker."

"Why, Daddy, you sly dog. You know Mama doesn't like it when you play poker. She says you get loose with your money and looser with your tongue."

"That's why I need you here. Make sure your old man stays in line." He nodded as if he was deadly serious. "If anything should go wrong, it will be your fault."

"Ha! Fine. But I don't think you'll be fooling Mama." Becky quickly finished her drink and stood from her favorite red chair. "I'll go see if Lucretia needs a hand."

"Rebecca Madeline, everyone knows you can't cook. Best leave that to the experts," Judge teased.

"I can watch, can't I?"

Becky was thrilled there would be some life at the house. If she knew Teddy Rockdale, he wouldn't come here for a gents' night without bringing Martha for her. Fanny would probably occupy herself by slinking around and boring anyone who would listen about Paris. But even the threat of more stories from overseas didn't dampen Becky's spirits. A party, even if it was a poker party, would be the bee's knees and just what the doctor ordered.

By the time the sun went down, Becky was dressed in one of her favorite party dresses. It was a simple frock, much more conservative than the black dress that had gotten ruined on the trip from 401 Portage Street. She pinned her hair back simply and wore a pair of her mother's ruby earbobs.

Of course, Fanny was wearing a scandalous ensemble, but everyone had gotten used to that. Well, perhaps not the fellas playing poker. As they arrived, they were all too happy to make her acquaintance and let her jabber on.

"I never saw anyone playing poker in Paris. Their

game was backgammon. A game of chance that the men took very seriously," she rambled on to some poor bloke Judge had invited from town. "I never learned it. Seemed a little too complicated for little old me."

Then, as if Becky wasn't already having a swell time listening to the music, chatting with Teddy, and indulging in the delicacies Lucretia had set out, a face she was shocked to see appeared in the foyer. Adam White was dressed in a sleek seersucker suit, his black curls swept back from his face. Becky had to stop and stare.

"What in the world are you doing here?" she asked as she walked over to escort him in.

"Your daddy invited me."

"He did?" Becky was beside herself. "Well, isn't that just the living end. Come on, I'll show you where the boys are set up. Teddy's here, so you won't be among total strangers."

As Becky escorted Adam into the parlor and made proper introductions, she looked at Lucretia, whose eyebrow went up with playful suspicion.

"Do you have something to say, Miss Lucretia?" Becky whispered as she took a platter of small sand-wiches from her.

The men were already getting boisterous, laughing, clapping each other on the back. The room filled with a thin haze of smoke before Moxley opened all the windows. A cool evening breeze wafted through the place and dragged the lace curtains by delicate, invisible fingertips, making the fabric wave and curl.

"No ma'am." Lucretia smirked. "Except that's a big fella. Who's goin' to do the cookin' if you two get hitched? Everyone knows you can't cook."

"Very funny. And no one's talking about getting hitched." Becky shook her head and straightened out the plates of food on the side table of the parlor.

"No one's talking. But the look on that man's face says he's seriously thinking it. Or at least thinking of the honeymoon." Lucretia chuckled.

"Lucretia!" Becky howled and laughed while shaking her head.

The poker game began after a few rounds of drinks. Becky winked at Adam before taking a champagne cocktail for herself and heading upstairs to get a little quiet for a few moments. This was a night for her daddy to unwind. After seeing Adam and Stephen fighting in the yard like a couple of schoolboys, she was thrilled Judge had let bygones be bygones. And she was glad Judge hadn't invited Stephen to attend the game. Sure, he was a dandy enough gent, but Becky believed what Adam had said. There was something about Stephen and Fanny that was getting under her skin. She took a seat on the edge of her bed and let out a deep breath.

What would she do when it was time to get hitched? She'd not be in her room anymore. The red wallpaper would be torn down for her mother to transform the room into a baby's playroom for the new grandchildren that would be expected within nine months of Becky saying "I do."

She looked at the glass in her hand and thought the idea of having a little bundle of joy would be very exciting... someday. And she would pray for a boy. Lord, she would be on her knees every night for a boy. If she had a girl, her worst nightmare would be an empty-headed bauble like Cousin Fanny. It would be her cross to bear for all the negative things she had ever said about the woman.

"Becky! Rebecca Madeline! Come down here!"

Becky heard her father shouting, snapping her out of her daydream. She tossed back the last of her drink and hurried downstairs. What she saw nearly made her choke.

"Becky, I've got someone I'd like you to meet," Judge said, standing in the foyer next to a man in a starched, stiff police uniform. "This is Officer Elby Ferris."

"Oh dear." Becky felt her breath come short. "I do hope the neighbors haven't called you on account of my father's rowdy party."

When the policeman turned around, she saw the same face that had corralled her just a few nights ago at the speakeasy behind the furniture store at 401 Portage.

"No ma'am." The officer extended his hand to Becky as if he'd never seen her before. "It's just a friendly call on your daddy."

"Can you pull up a chair for a quick game? How about a little toot for the road?" Judge asked innocently.

"Oh, thank you, no, Judge. I was just in the neighborhood and thought I'd stop by. After we talked this afternoon, I thought I'd just skirt by the plantation to see the crops and give a friendly howdy-do," Officer Ferris said. "My goodness, your daughter is lovely. She must take after the wife."

Becky smiled nervously and fidgeted with the hem of her frock. Was this officer of the law really unaware she'd run into him at a rather rough speakeasy just a few nights ago, or was he playing her for a fool? Maybe he knew exactly who she was. Maybe this was just for show. A threat to make her keep her mouth shut about... what? That he'd had one too many at an illegal speakeasy? That was a crime committed by more than seventy percent of the population in Savannah on a nightly basis. Of course she wouldn't squeal. Even if she wanted to, who would she tell? The police?

"Thank you, Officer. Are you sure I can't get you a drink?" Becky offered, regaining her footing. If this was a game, she had no choice but to play along. "The ice is exceptionally cold tonight."

"My, she is a charmer," Officer Ferris said. "You talked me into it."

"Good." Judge clapped him on the back. "Becky, scare up a martini, or maybe he'd like a scotch. And pack up a slice of pie for him to take on the road."

"Yes, Daddy," Becky said and sauntered into the parlor.

Adam had been watching the whole thing transpire, but he didn't move or act as if there was anything out of order. Becky was glad he was there. Because even though Officer Ferris acted polite, even though his eyes weren't feverish or glassy anymore and he wasn't sweating as if he'd just chased a bank robber for eight blocks, there was still something in his demeanor that left Becky feeling vulnerable. It was as if someone had barged into the water closet while she was washing up before bed.

He was in her home and peeking into her life uninvited.

Adam finally walked up behind Becky to help himself to a fresh drink. "Are you all right?" he asked while pretending he was studying the bottles of hooch.

"Tell me you remember that man talking with my father," Becky said with a sweet smile on her face.

"He'd be hard to forget. I think it's no coincidence that he's here," Adam added. "But I can honestly say I don't know what to do about it. He's behind a shield made of one hundred percent copper. It wouldn't be wise for any of us to say or do anything."

"What could he want?" Becky asked.

"Maybe he just wants to see if we remember him. Or maybe he wants to make sure we'll keep quiet about what we know. It's hard to tell," Adam said before helping himself to a slice of pie and taking a bite so big half of the slice was gone in an instant.

Becky couldn't help but remember Lucretia's words about cooking. She was going to be in dire straits if she didn't learn a couple tricks to keep Adam's belly full. What an odd thought to have at this moment. Adam winked at Becky and returned to the table, where Teddy was talking fast as he dealt the next hand.

As Becky fixed a drink and wrapped a slice of pie in a couple of napkins, she listened to Judge and the officer talking.

"So, you say your kin hail from Alabama. My wife is visiting her own kin in Alabama right now," Judge offered.

"Oh, I do hope it isn't anything serious," Officer Ferris replied.

"Family drama. It flares up in those parts once every blue moon, and, well, you know how family can be." Judge guffawed.

"I do have a sister who has a long line of dramatic encounters with her in-laws. So far, I've escaped the preacher. However, after seeing your daughter, I may have to rethink my devotion to bachelorhood."

Becky pretended she didn't hear a word and walked up to her father. "I hope you like pecan pie. Even if you don't, Lucretia's pies will convert you faster than a priest on Easter Sunday." Becky smiled.

"Well, thank you kindly, Miss Rebecca. I do appreciate it." Officer Elby Ferris looked directly at Becky. His eyes flashed as they travelled over her face and down her neck before popping back to her eyes again.

"Judge! It's your hand!" the men at the poker table started shouting.

"Uncle Judge, you want me to play your hand for you?" Teddy shouted.

"You get your hands off my cards, boy!" Judge shouted back.

"I'm sorry, Judge. I certainly didn't mean to keep you from your game. You and the boys have a pleasant evening. Perhaps your lovely daughter could escort me to my car. I'd hate to abscond with your wife's lovely crystal, but I also don't want the contents to go to waste." Officer Ferris raised the crystal tumbler filled halfway with ice and gin.

Everyone laughed. Judge clapped Officer Ferris on the back, heartily shaking his hand before returning to the poker table.

"After you, Officer." Becky smiled as she held the screen door open.

"By all means." He stood back, letting Becky walk ahead of him.

A shiver ran across her spine, as she was sure he was looking at her with the most ungentlemanly of intentions. Whether he remembered her or not, a leopard didn't change its spots. Becky cleared her throat as she turned to look at the officer before descending the front porch steps.

"It sure was nice of you to stop by, Officer. Daddy is a real talker. You're lucky you got out of there as quickly as you did. One more mint julep, and you might have been lassoed into hearing his tobacco tales. I do hope you have a safe evening and—"

"You can quit pretending, Miss Rebecca. We're alone now," Officer Ferris said.

It was as if a different person had slipped into his uniform. Maybe it was the shadows playing tricks, maybe it was just the soft porch lighting, but Officer Elby Ferris had transformed from an average copper to an awkward, tittering young man. He tossed the drink she'd made in the dirt and handed Becky her mother's fine crystal glass.

"Pretending? Why, that was perfectly good gin you just threw away. Why don't you let me get you another and—"

"The truth is I'm not a big drinker. Sometimes I lose my head and, well, while I'm still on duty, I can't have that happen. I was just trying to be polite to your daddy. Now tell me what an upstanding, law-abiding man like Judge Mackenzie is doing with a daughter that sneaks around looking in places she's not been invited to. Hmm?"

Becky's heart lodged in her throat. She looked at

the front door. It seemed so far away. The men were talking and chiding one another. She could hear it through the window, but they might as well have been a hundred miles away.

"Just get the idea of telling your daddy anything right out of your pretty little head," Officer Ferris said. He took a step closer and inhaled deeply, as if he was smelling the soap on her skin. "I'm not here to harm you. I'm here to help. You are in grave danger, and it isn't from me. I think you know who's been looking for you."

"What are you talking about?" Becky's words were less than convincing.

"A certain big palooka thinks you've got a trinket that belongs to him. Do you have it?" The policeman kicked the dirt in front of him as if he were just shooting the breeze with a pretty girl.

"Have what? A trinket? I've got lots of them."

"Now come clean, Miss Becky. I saw you. Leonard Brennan wasn't the only fella who had his eye on you. You're just lucky I got to you before he did." Officer Ferris licked his lips and smiled. He looked quite boyish and playful, like this was a game and he was having fun.

"I wish I could help you, Officer. But I really don't know what you are talking about."

To say Becky was confused was an understatement. But she didn't dare ask for any clarification. What could she say? Was the good officer talking about the time she illegally broke into Violet's apartment and was snooping around? Or was he talking about the time they saw each other at the rough-and-tumble speakeasy? Or was he referring to something else? If she let on about anything, she felt he'd have her cornered. So she played dumb.

"I'll tell you what. You think about it." He cleared his throat and smiled. "You think long and hard, and then you meet me at the Cadillac Diner on Fifth Avenue tomorrow at noon. Lunch will be on me."

"But Officer Ferris, I can tell you that I really don't know what you're talking about. If you saw me at some speakeasy, well, I was probably lit before I got there. I have a blurry memory more often than I'd like to admit." She chuckled nervously. "In fact, I don't even remember where I went last night. I sure hope I had a good time."

"You didn't go anywhere last night, darlin'. Or the night before," he purred. "Meet me tomorrow at the Cadillac Diner."

"And what if I decide to pay a visit to Leonard Brennan instead and ask him why I've got a copper telling me I need to be careful of him? He was the main squeeze of a good friend of mine." Becky batted her lashes as if she were the epitome of innocence.

"I wouldn't suggest that. He's under investigation for the murder of his girlfriend. I'm sure you heard about what happened to her. If he did that to someone he loves, what's to stop him from doing it to someone he barely knows?" Officer Ferris asked. "Leonard Brennan is a monster. He's connected to some of the most notorious characters in town, and they don't give a whip about how sweet a girl might be or how affluent her father is."

Becky swallowed hard and listened to her father laughing and telling a corny joke that made the men guffaw and howl.

"Meet me tomorrow, and we can talk about how we are going to make sure Leonard Brennan pays for his crimes. It's your duty as a Christian and as a law-abiding citizen. Besides, I think it would be just ducky to have a little time to get to know you. Those rumors I hear can't all be true. Why, you look like the kind of girl any man would be proud to bring home to Mama." He smiled as if he'd just given her the best compliment ever uttered. So why did Becky feel as if he had just given her a smack? Officer Ferris tipped his hat with the silver medallion on it and walked to the driver's-side door. "See you tomorrow. And please don't make me come looking for you."

Becky stood on the dirt driveway and watched as the police car turned around and headed out the way it had come. What was she going to do?

Fanny appeared in the front door. "Who was that?"

Becky thought her cousin must have been losing her touch, because a man had come and gone without her knowledge.

"Just a friend of Daddy's," Becky muttered.

"And you didn't think to introduce me? Why, Rebecca, your mama would be ashamed of how your manners just slip out the door the minute she's away." Fanny huffed and went back into the house.

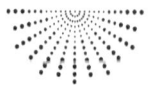

# CHAPTER THIRTEEN

*T*he next day, Becky hitched a ride with one of the nearby farmers into town. The sky was a perfectly clear blue, with just a couple of white puffy clouds lazily drifting by with no intention of covering up the sun for any length of time. After a good night's sleep that followed seeing Adam and Judge getting along so well, Becky faced her appointment with Officer Ferris with a new set of eyes. Perhaps he really was willing to help. She certainly knew what side of the law he was on compared to Leonard Brennan, and after seeing what Brennan had done to Violet on so many occasions, she figured she could use a friend with a badge.

*But what about his behavior at the speakeasy?* That

little voice in the back of Becky's mind just didn't want to let go. It nagged and pinched and twisted her thoughts until she thought she'd scream. He had looked like a crazed lunatic that night. And there was that girl who had slipped into that room with him. And Miss Chantilly. Becky thought that woman probably held the secrets of half the Brunos in town, along with the mayor, the chief of police, the head of the Ezekiel Baptist Church, and who knew who else.

*He could have been on a bender. He wouldn't be the first guy to get tough after a few shots of liquid courage. He certainly wouldn't be the last.* It was easy to convince herself that Officer Ferris was as nice as he had seemed at her home. But as Becky entered the Cadillac Diner on Fifth Avenue, her palms got wet and her mouth went dry. She'd experienced this feeling a hundred times during her school days when she'd asked an unusual question or made what the teachers dubbed a "smart observation," meaning she was being rude. She'd been held back after class or sent to the principal's office to have a discussion about her attitude. That was exactly what she felt like now. Officer Ferris was going to ask her about some trinket, and when she denied having it, he was going to tell her that he didn't like her attitude and that it would get her into trouble and that with an attitude like hers, there would be a long, lonely life ahead of her.

"Becky!" a female voice called.

As if her luck couldn't have been any worse, Becky turned to see Ellen-Lyn Merriweather on the other side of the diner in a booth with three other women from the Ladies' Auxiliary, gawking at her as if she was on display at the zoo. Ellen-Lyn was waving madly with a look on her face like she was watching a tightrope walker she was hoping would fall. Becky didn't know what was worse, facing Officer Ferris alone or facing him with Ellen-Lyn Merriweather just a couple booths over, taking notes to read back to Kitty.

"Hello, Mrs. Merriweather. Ladies," Becky said politely.

"I heard your poor mother had to rush off to Mississippi to tend to one of her infirm relatives. How is she doing?" Mrs. Merriweather rooted out details like pigs did truffles.

"She's in Alabama. We expect her back soon," Becky replied.

"So, what are you doing here?" Ellen-Lyn asked.

"Having lunch. I assume you are taking the county census?" Becky teased. "If anyone can collect the details about a town, it's you."

Mrs. Merriweather smiled and stared at Becky before chuckling. "Well, you tell your mama that I will be looking forward to a nice long visit to catch up as soon as she gets back. Oh, and tell her to bring that Fanny Doshoffer. She is such a charming girl. A real jewel in the family crown."

"Yes, ma'am," Becky replied.

After wishing the ladies a delightful lunch, she turned to find an empty booth to sit in. She'd almost forgotten why she was even at this particular diner on the other side of town. But it only took a second when she saw Officer Ferris, his uniform heavily starched and clean. He took off his hat, tucked it under his arm, and looked around the place. Becky wondered if she should wave to him. Should she call his name? Thankfully, she didn't have to do either. He spied her, smiled, and casually walked toward her.

"I am so glad to see you," he murmured.

"Really?" Becky studied Officer Ferris's face. In the bright light of day, he looked like a Boy Scout ready to do his duty for God and country.

"Honest Abe." He put up his hand as if he was swearing an oath. No good Southerner would ever use that specific expression, but she wasn't about to correct the man with the badge and gun in front of her. "Mind if I sit?"

"Officer, what is this really about?" she asked as he slid into the seat across from her.

Within an instant the waitress was over, smiling and chatting with him like they were old friends. She poured two cups of coffee without being asked and told them she would be back in a jiffy to take their order. Becky would have preferred a lemonade, but now was not the time to complain.

"Please, call me Elby. We're going to be good friends, and friends don't call me Officer Ferris. You know, they have a wonderful biscuits and gravy here that will knock your socks off." He continued to smile.

"Officer… Elby, aren't we here to discuss something?" Becky looked around the diner and slumped when she confirmed that Ellen-Lyn and the other hens were watching her with interest. Kitty was going to flip when she got wind of her daughter sitting with a police officer.

"Don't you want to have lunch first? I'm starved," he replied as he studied the menu.

"I can't say I've got much of an appetite," Becky admitted.

"Oh, you poor thing. I worried you last night

talking about Leonard Brennan, didn't I? Well, you're right to be worried about him. But not while I'm here."

He winked. Becky felt as if she was in a strange dream. But it was about to get stranger, because a dark shadow seemed to walk right through the door of the restaurant.

At first, Becky thought the beautiful day was perhaps changing and a cloud bank had decided to roll in. But when she looked out the window, everything was as sunny as it had been. Perhaps a lightbulb had suddenly burned out. Restaurants had to go through them as frequently as eggs, since they were on all day long. Casually, she looked up and saw every bulb overhead glowing.

But when she looked toward the door, there was something clouding the entrance. No one else seemed to notice it. The patrons continued eating, chatting, or reading their papers. Becky tried to ignore it, chalking it up to just a trick of the light. But as the dark, shadowy column slithered in her direction, she felt a chill in the air. It stopped at the edge of the table and hovered there as Elby spoke. He, like the rest of the diners, didn't see it.

"So, Becky, I've learned through some of my sources on the street that Leonard Brennan killed

Violet Darcy. In fact, everyone knows it. The problem is that he has an alibi. Of course he does, right? Guys like him always solidify their whereabouts when doing the Devil's work."

Becky was only half listening to him as she watched the black shadow that no one else noticed begin to twitch and bend and writhe around as if it were somehow in pain even though it wasn't a person or an animal. It was a shadow.

"He killed that poor girl by putting a bullet in the back of her head," Elby said.

The words snapped at Becky, grabbing her attention. She looked at Elby's face. He was calm and cool, with his collar buttoned to the very top, his navy-blue uniform jacket smooth, without a trace of lint, and those copper buttons winking in the light. Becky found the shiny copper buttons to be almost hypnotic. They blinked and flashed with even the tiniest shift in Elby's position. But suddenly they, too, were snuffed out by the shadow. It swept over him like some kind of protective shroud. Becky heard Elby's voice become far off, as if he was shouting at her down a long tunnel. The sounds of clanking dishes and silverware, the conversations among the patrons, the ping of the bell at the counter for a pick-up, and the soft hum of the ceiling fans overhead were almost completely gone. All Becky could hear was Elby's voice. This shadow wanted Becky to hear every word. But not because the shadow agreed with him; that became apparent quickly.

After swallowing hard, Becky watched as the blackness settled over Elby. His face twitched when he blinked as if an eyelash had become a serious problem, poking at the delicate orb. The corners of his mouth drew down, and his cheeks sank into deep shadows. Darkness whirled around his head, but his hair, cropped short on the sides and just a little longer on top, remained motionless.

"The reason I need your help is because my sources on the street also tell me that you were seen coming out of the victim's apartment."

Those words snapped at Becky like a schoolboy shooting her with a rubber band. Instantly, she focused on Elby's eyes. They were saying much more than his kind-sounding words. They were dark and intense, studying her. Whatever this shadow was, it was clinging to Elby like sweat.

"You had something in your hand. I think it is exactly what will prove that Leonard Brennan killed her. You see, she gave him a gift from a jewelry store. That jeweler will testify that Violet had that made for him and that she didn't have it in her possession until the day she was killed. I know it sounds a little far-fetched, but believe me when I tell you that little item will close this case and close the bars on Leonard Brennan for a long, long time."

At those words, the black mist became even darker, like a swarm of bees, around his face and shoulders. For a few seconds, the right side of his face was covered, making the left side look pale and sickly. Then it shifted, and the lower half of his face was covered, leaving the top part looking ghostly.

"Are you all right, darling?" Elby asked Becky. "You look like you've just seen a ghost. Goodness, it is chilly in here. I think we must be sitting beneath a draft of some kind."

Becky swallowed again, knowing what was giving Elby the heebie-jeebies. But what *exactly* was it?

Finally, the thing froze as if it had heard Becky's thoughts. Within a split second, it shot up to the ceiling and back toward the door, where a patron stepping inside tripped and lost his balance. He fell to the ground, drawing the attention of every person in the place.

The waitress who had waited on Becky's table rushed over to him and helped him to his feet, along with a couple other folks who had been seated at the counter just a few steps away. He seemed no worse for wear, but the black thing, whatever it was, was now gone.

"That alderman probably dipped the bill once too often before his lunch break." Elby laughed at the poor man, who was red-faced and apologetic to everyone around.

"He just tripped. He could have cracked his kisser," Becky replied sympathetically. Something in her gut, aside from the mysterious black mist that had surrounded Elby, made her feel he wasn't telling her the whole story. If only she could talk to Leonard and get his side of the story without him killing her.

"So, do you still have the little item that I'm looking for?" Elby finally asked.

"I really don't know. It's true I was at Violet's apartment. She was my friend, although it was pretty casual. But I honestly can't recall if I have anything of hers. She had quite expensive tastes that would look rather garish on me." Becky fluttered her lashes and shrugged innocently.

"Now I wouldn't say that. I think I know of several gents who'd be willing to test that theory with a new fur or a string of diamonds." Elby smiled back just as innocently.

"Are you flirting with me, Elby?" Becky asked, hoping her straightforwardness might knock him off balance.

"Flirting with you? Well, you got me. When I found out Judge Mackenzie had a daughter, I was intrigued. When I got a look at you, I'll admit, I was smitten." He peeled his lips back from his teeth in a strange way. It was almost as if he wasn't smiling but baring his teeth. "Do you think maybe, if you look around your bedroom tonight, you might find that little item I'm inquiring about? I'll bet you have a real pretty room with one of those four-poster beds."

Becky had kissed Adam White passionately and often but would have slapped his handsome face if he ever spoke of her most intimate sanctuary in such a way. The tone in Elby's voice and the fire behind his eyes made Becky shiver. He chuckled.

"I will be happy to look, Elby," Becky said, looking at the clock over the counter. "Oh dear. Is that really the time? I'm afraid I'll have to cut our visit short, Elby."

"But you haven't had anything to eat. Just wait, and I'll order you an ice cream cone," Elby said earnestly.

"Perhaps another time," Becky said, quickly scooting out of the booth, nearly running right into the man who had fallen upon entering the diner. "I do promise to look for this particular item you have mentioned. If I find it, should I contact the precinct?"

"No!" Elby almost shouted. "You don't want to talk to the boys there. They'll think you are making a phony phone call or playing some kind of flim-flam."

"All right. What should I do if I find I do indeed have what you are searching for?" Becky asked, hoping that her voice didn't tremble too much. She had a bad feeling in her gut and wanted to get out of there as quickly as possible. Funny how that dark, ominous shadow had been an enigma, but while it had been present, Becky hadn't felt scared. With it gone, she wanted to do nothing but run away.

"Why don't you call me directly." Elby pulled a card from his pocket. "You can reach me at this number. If I'm not there, you can leave word, and my associates will make sure to pass along your message." It wasn't a card from the police station. It was just a plain white piece of stock paper with a number on it. Not even his name was listed.

"This is a very strange calling card." Becky heard the words slip out before she could stop them.

"You think so?" he replied, the smile starting to fade from his face.

"I promise to call if I find it. You enjoy your lunch, Officer Ferris," Becky said loudly and quickly hurried out the door. The only things she was sure of were that Elby Ferris was the one attempting a flim-flam, and Ellen-Lyn Merriweather would be giving Kitty Mackenzie an earful.

# CHAPTER FOURTEEN

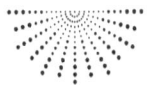

*I*t had been more than a year ago that Becky had had the incident with her father's car that had prevented her from getting behind the wheel of any automobile since. People who didn't know her assumed that she'd gotten into some kind of accident that resulted in her father paying for damages and prohibiting Becky from ever driving again. Becky only wished her "incident" had been that simple.

The truth was that the poor girl had realized how much different it was sitting in the driver's seat than the passenger's seat. She'd ridden shotgun a million times with Moxley and Judge, and Teddy would have made a fortune if he were paid by the trip as Becky's personal chauffeur. She'd never had the slightest feeling of discomfort, not even a pinch of hesitation, any time she climbed into someone's automobile.

"Darlin', how about you take us home," Judge had said one quiet afternoon after they'd driven to the very edge of the plantation to inspect the crops.

"Really?" Becky was thrilled. She hadn't ever driven a vehicle, but she'd been paying close attention, asking questions and in every way possible making it clear to her father that she was anxious to learn to drive.

"The dirt road is quiet enough. I think you can give it the old college try without threat of injury to yourself or your dear old daddy." Judge smiled.

Without hesitating, Becky hopped into the driver's seat. Judge took his place in the passenger's seat and calmly instructed his daughter on how to get the engine purring.

"You're a natural," he said as she quickly got the engine to turn over.

"I've been paying attention to you and Moxley. When you shift the gears, you hit the clutch then ease off real gently and tap the gas. It's just like learning a new dance," she said with her chin raised.

"Well then, take me to your mother." Judge smiled and pointed off down the road.

It was true that Becky had the car under control

like she'd been born to drive. But as she moved down the dirt road, Judge noticed something peculiar about his daughter. She was turning green around the gills.

"Honey, are you all right?" he asked.

She nodded quickly and forced a smile. "Sure, Daddy. I'm just trying to concentrate. That's all."

But that *wasn't* all. Becky's hands were the first things to get clammy. She wiped them one at a time on the front of her dungarees. Then sweat started to form on her forehead and down the center of her back, while at the same time a chill ran across her shoulders. Her stomach felt as if there was a giant raw egg rolling around inside it. With every jerk of the steering wheel or dip in the dirt road, she felt it rise and fall, higher and higher up her throat.

"Becky, honey, I think you should stop the car," Judge said.

"I'm okay, Daddy," Becky muttered from between lips pinched so tightly together they were white.

"I really think you should pull over and let me drive," Judge said.

"I'll be all right, Daddy. Every girl I know drives a car," she protested, shaking her head and blinking to focus.

"Now, Rebecca, I'm telling you to stop this car before—"

Becky did stop the car. She slammed on the brakes and brought the machine to an abrupt halt just before she threw up all over the steering wheel. Judge had to use his cotton jacket and his favorite tailored shirt to clean up and cover the mess in order to get the car home. The front of Becky's blouse was ruined. She stomped angrily into the house, ignoring her mother's questions, and slammed her bedroom door. That night over dinner, Judge had had a few things to say.

"I think the surprise of having to drive might have just overwhelmed you," he soothed. "Plus, you had gone out last evening, and heaven knows what you might have had to drink that perhaps didn't resolve itself by morning."

Becky peeked up from beneath her lashes at her father and felt her cheeks rage in embarrassment.

"I say that we plan for you to try again tomorrow. We'll have a nice discussion about the procedure. You certainly seemed to know how to handle the machine. We'll just have a nice time and relax, and I'll bet you'll be picking out your own flivver within the month."

That made Becky feel a world of better. The next

day after Judge finished with his paperwork and tasks in the field, he found Becky swinging on the porch swing. At that same time, Martha and Teddy came walking along the path that connected the two bits of property, carrying a bottle of champagne each.

"It's a beautiful night. We thought we'd spend it over here. And besides, Mother has her cousins from Okeydoke, Wisconsin, visiting. I can hardly understand a word they are saying because their Midwestern accents are so strong," Teddy said.

"Well, y'all just make yourselves comfortable on the porch, and Daddy and I'll be right back. He's teaching me to drive," Becky said confidently. But her insides weren't so sure she'd be able to make it this time either.

Within minutes, Judge had pulled the car around from the barn and had Becky hop in the passenger's side. She looked fine. She felt fine. Within the next few minutes, she was sure she'd be steering her daddy's car up to the house for Teddy and Martha to hop in and join her and head off to the nearest juke joint.

But things don't always turn out the way they're planned. And after being gone for only ten minutes, Judge came driving the car back up the long dirt driveway in his T-shirt, with his jacket covering the driver's seat and his second-favorite tailored shirt over the steering wheel. As soon as they got to the house, Becky got out of the car, her second blouse ruined and her pride nowhere to be found.

"How did it go?" Teddy asked. "Why, Becky, did you have an accident?"

"Yes!" she shouted as she stomped into the house. Martha had gone to talk with Lucretia and had missed Becky's return. Even Teddy wasn't sure what had happened, and he got no indication from Judge, who angrily drove the car back to the barn.

It was decided that although Becky had no problem being the passenger in any automobile, she suffered severe motion sickness and anxiety when behind the wheel. Judge had tried to cure her of her malady, which he believed was all in her head, but with no luck.

So when Becky needed to get somewhere and there was no chariot waiting, she quickly learned to thumb a ride. Today was one of those days.

A driver hauling peaches was happy to give Becky a lift, and she was thrilled to sit in the back of the truck, inhaling the sweet perfume of the ripe fruits. She managed to slip one into her pocket before waving goodbye to the kind man. She ate the juicy thing and sucked on the pit as she strolled to Madame Cecelia's store.

"Well, this is a nice surprise." Madame Cecelia smiled as Becky walked in, setting off the tinkling chimes over the door. Ophelia, Cecelia's mother, grunted her salutation. "I was expecting you sooner. What took you so long?"

"What do you mean you were expecting me?" Becky huffed.

"I had my tea this morning. Saw it at the bottom of the cup." She winked at Becky before waving for her to follow her upstairs. "You're bringing me a ball and chain to look at."

"A ball and chain? What are you talking about?" Becky asked as she followed Cecelia into her apartment.

It smelled nice, like cloves, and the sun was filtering through the plants that sat in the windows. The leaves of a couple of droopy ferns hung over their pots, and interspersed between them were some odd but beautiful plants that Becky was sure held some kind of strange power. There wasn't anything in Cecelia's home that didn't appear mysterious even though the day was bright.

"You're carrying something very heavy in your

pocket," Cecelia said as she walked to the small stove and put the kettle on.

"No. Just this," Becky said, pulling the silver flask from under her skirt. She'd tucked it beneath her garter and had barely noticed it was there.

Cecelia's face became somber as she took the thing from Becky. She turned it around in her hands and looked at the inscription. But before she handed it back to Becky, she sniffled.

"There is a lot of sadness over this item," she said. "I don't know how you were able to carry it and not feel it. It's so heavy, like it's filled with cement or lead."

"I think someone is looking for it," Becky said as if the words were painful coming out of her mouth. Quickly, she told Cecelia how she'd come across the little item and that she was afraid that the person, LB, Leonard Brennan, was looking for her.

"For someone who has the gift of sight and can communicate with spirits that have passed on, I am shocked at how little you know about things." Cecelia walked over to her bookshelf. "I think it's time for your lessons to really begin."

"My lessons?" Becky asked.

"Oh, I'm sorry. What have you got to do with your time besides go dancing with that handsome

Adam fellow and fight with your cousin?" Cecelia replied without turning around.

"I'll have you know I've got plenty to do. Like figure out what I'm supposed to do with this flask and how I can help Violet. She's trying to tell me something. But I'm not picking up what she's putting down."

Becky felt so much better talking with Cecelia. The words she was saying would have made her own mother faint or call some doctor to have her committed to the booby hatch for sure. Martha was a gem, but even she wouldn't know what to say about all this. Cecelia understood. To her, none of what Becky was saying was weird or scary or abnormal.

"Here, take this book. Read the chapter on transference and then tell me what you get from your little item here," Cecelia said, handing Becky a book with a faded purple cover and old brown pages.

Becky held it to her nose and inhaled deeply. She loved the smell of old books. "You aren't going to tell me?" Becky asked hopefully.

"Someday I may not be here. You've got to learn to solve these mysteries yourself," Cecelia said.

"Well, that's a cheerful thought. You're not hiding something from me?" Becky had come to rely on

Cecelia when her own strange ability was leading her somewhere she was afraid to go.

"I don't know. Am I?" Cecelia raised her eyebrow.

"Very funny. No, I don't think so," Becky said, squinting.

"I will tell you this. The last person to touch this before you was carrying a very heavy burden. He or she knew something that was dangerous. I think this was a woman. Am I right?" Cecelia asked.

Becky nodded.

"That explains the image I keep getting. Flowers. Purple."

"Her name was Violet," Becky replied.

Cecelia smiled and shook her head. "It wasn't just a single issue. She'd been carrying things with her her whole life. And the one thing she thought could help her turned out to be the biggest burden of all. Oh, but wait." Cecelia rubbed the smooth surface and unscrewed the top, taking a sniff of what had been inside. "She was making one last-ditch effort when she last held this. Something was about to change. But I can't see anything after that."

Becky took the flask and held it. When she cleared her mind, she felt a slight vibration but nothing more.

"I guess I need to read the book. I'm coming up with nothing," she admitted.

"That's okay, Becky," Cecelia said as she went back to the tea on the stove.

After a few more minutes both women were sitting at the table with their steaming cups of tea in front of them. Cecelia was telling Becky about when she was a young girl. Becky held the flask, which was resting on the book she was to read. It still vibrated ever so slightly in her hand.

## CHAPTER FIFTEEN

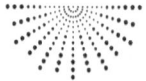

"You don't know how happy I am that you came to my rescue," Becky said as she took hold of Adam's hand. "If I'd spent another night under my daddy's roof, I'd have just about blown a gasket."

"Well, I'm glad I could oblige," Adam said as they strolled down one of the main drags in the city. Saturday night in downtown Savannah was jumping and jiving. Flappers and Shebas hung off the arms of their butter-and-egg men with short, wide ties and two-toned shoes as they slipped from one dive that had peanut shells on the floor to another that was a clip joint. Keeping track of them all was like trying to see the beautiful carved animals on a carousel before they spun past.

Becky and Adam had hit three speakeasies, danced five dances, drunk half a dozen champagne cocktails between the two of them, said hello to at least twenty people Becky knew by name, and finally had a chance just to shoot the breeze and cool off with a stroll down the avenue.

"I still can't believe what that Officer Elby Ferris was saying to me," Becky rambled. "He was certainly trying to sell me something, but I wasn't buying. He knew that too. I don't think he cared."

"I can't believe you went without telling me or anyone else where you were headed. Do you know how dangerous that was?" Adam said, slipping his arm around Becky's waist. "Not all the coppers in this town are on the up-and-up."

"Oh, it was broad daylight. I wasn't afraid," Becky huffed.

"Of course you weren't. That's your problem. You've seen things that would scare normal people, so you are immune to actual scary situations. Like meeting a stranger for lunch," Adam said, holding his chin high. "You need someone around to tell you when to be calm and when to be afraid."

"You think you're so smart." Becky snuggled closer to him. She walked with her head against his shoulder for a couple of paces then spoke again. "Adam, I have to tell you something important."

"This sounds serious," he replied.

"I feel I have to tell you that I can't cook." Becky spat the words out quickly.

"You can't cook? Um... neither can I?" Adam replied, looking down at her curiously.

"I can't cook. I'm okay at keeping things tidy, but I am wary of going into places with cobwebs or dust bunnies. I don't think I've looked under my bed in years." She smiled. "I don't think I've ever ironed a single piece of clothing. Golly, I sound rather useless." Becky frowned.

"Useless? You?" Adam removed his arm from around her waist and offered her his elbow. She slipped her hand through and squeezed his strong biceps.

"Rebecca Madeline Mackenzie, who makes sure everyone has a full glass at every party? Who makes sure every lonely heart gets at least one turn on the dance floor? And might I just inquire who treats everyone, whether they are a lowly doorman or hatcheck girl or proprietor of the swankiest joint in Savannah, the same, with a flirty remark and an inviting smile? I never thought I'd hope to be hand-cuffed to the most popular gal in town. Never in my life." Adam's chest swelled with pride. "Yet here I am, willing to renounce Abe Lincoln and snow on Christmas, all for you."

Becky looked up at him, the streetlights making her eyes twinkle. "So, you don't mind if I can't cook?"

"No, Becky. I don't mind," Adam said.

"You wouldn't rather have someone like Fanny?" Becky teased.

"Can she cook?" Adam asked.

"If she can, she's hiding it from us," Becky snapped.

"She's ugly," Adam said, pulling his lips down into a frown and squinting.

"Now I know you are lying." Becky chuckled.

But when Adam stopped and looked down at her, she felt a wave of excitement she'd never experienced before. They were on a lively sidewalk. There were a couple of great speakeasies on this particular block, small, intimate places where a couple could neck in peace without the Mrs. Merriweathers of the world spying and reporting what they'd seen to everyone. However, Becky didn't want to leave the spot she was in. Adam smoothed her red hair away from her face. His hands were rough but warm against her cheek. He stood close, took her hand in his, and tugged her down three steps into a gangway that was completely concealed in shadows.

Once off the main street and hidden from view, Adam slipped his arms around Becky, pulled her to him tighter than he ever had before, and gazed at her face. Her breath came out in a gasp. She was on her toes, leaning into his broad chest, when he kissed her breath away. Every thought in her head was kissed away. His soft lips and the spicy smell of his skin made Becky feel like she was floating. The sound of hard-bottomed shoes scuffing the sidewalk, people's voices mingled together, and honking car horns were the music to their private dance.

When Adam finally pulled his lips away from Becky's, she could still feel his hot breath against her neck. She put her hands to his chest and, through the fabric of his work shirt, felt his heart pounding madly.

The door above them opened and slammed shut as the owner of the two-flat came outside. He descended the stairs, just inches from Becky and Adam, who watched through the spaces of the wooden steps, hoping he didn't decide to turn down the gangway and catch them. Instead, the man wearing brown-and-white shoes stopped at the bottom of the stoop, lit a cigarette, then dropped the smoldering match to the sidewalk and strolled off.

"I love you, Becky. Since the minute I first saw you," Adam whispered in her ear, sending shivers up her spine.

She leaned into him and squeezed him tighter in her arms. "I love you too."

They kissed again, letting the nightlife continue without them for just a little while longer. With their eyes adjusted to the darkness, they whispered their secrets to one another, promising never to tell, to keep their words and actions just between them. When Becky looked up at Adam, she smoothed back the black curls that had fallen forward across his forehead. She ran her hand down his cheek, feeling the stubble that had deliciously scratched her skin. And just as she looked up to kiss him one more time, stomping footsteps gave her pause.

"Where did they go? They were just here." The sound of two gruff voices cut through Becky and Adam's special moment. "I saw them with my own eyes. Small redhead with her police dog at her side."

"It's impossible to lose a guy as big as that palooka. And her hair is so red you can't miss her."

It was obvious to Becky and Adam these men were talking about them. Adam slowly released

Becky from his arms and put his index finger to his lips. Becky nodded. They quietly turned and looked through the openings between the stairs as they had just a few minutes ago.

"I like redheads," one man with a fedora said as he twisted his pinky ring.

"Yeah, I'll take a blonde any day. Hey, if we go back to the boss and tell him we lost them, he's not going to be happy," the fella with the trench coat said.

"Look, I don't know about you, but I just did a stint at Chatham. I'm in no hurry to go back. These chumps obviously did something to upset the boss. But all I agreed to was a tail. If he wants anything more, he'll have to find his own button man," Pinky Ring said.

"Look, he's paying us, isn't he?" Trench Coat replied.

"Uh-oh. Speak of the devil. Look who's coming."

Adam and Becky carefully peeked around the brick wall that was giving them cover and saw the two guys step up to a car that had just pulled alongside the curb. It wasn't just any car. It was a police car. Becky gasped, bit her lip, and looked up at Adam. She knew exactly who was in that car: Officer

Elby Ferris. Adam shook his head and squeezed her shoulders reassuringly.

"They were just here. You know there's a club every couple of feet in this neighborhood. They had to have just ducked in somewhere," the man with the fedora and pinky ring said.

"Hey! Hey, pal!" The driver's side door of the police car opened, and a very familiar-looking police officer stepped out. He hurried around the front of the car to a tall, thin gent who was minding his own business, strolling down the sidewalk.

"You see a couple walk by? A big guy with clodhopper boots and a gal with bright-red hair? They were going this way?" The police officer pointed down the sidewalk.

"No, Officer. I didn't see anyone. What did they do?" the wiry fellow asked.

"None of your business," Officer Ferris snapped. He acted nothing like the guy who had sat at the Cadillac Diner, chatting pleasantly with the waitress and trying to sweet-talk Becky.

"All right, Officer. No need to get sore," the thin man whined.

"You can move along before I slap the cuffs on you for loitering," Officer Ferris said before walking up to Mr. Trench Coat and Mr. Pinky Ring, who had been following Becky and Adam for who knew how long before the couple had accidentally ditched them.

"Look, Elby, they were right here. They couldn't have gotten far," one of them said as he worried his pinky ring.

"Elby," Becky whispered. "Officer Elby Ferris. The policeman we saw that night when Leonard Brennan was chasing us. The policeman who showed up at my house. Who I saw today."

She felt Adam's strong arms tighten around her, but even that didn't bring her any comfort. Everyone knew that there was no arguing against the law. If a man in a uniform said you were a criminal, then by gosh, you were a criminal. If you were shot dead in the street, you were the one in the wrong place at the wrong time. Of course, Becky knew not all the coppers were like this. Most were really good eggs just making a living and trying to keep the streets safe. But she'd have been a fool to think there weren't a few Elby Ferrises infiltrating the rank and file. And once one of them decided they had a beef with you, there were only two options. A person could dust out and become a bindle stiff, hopping the first open train car to parts unknown, or become a sitting duck while waiting for a wooden kimono.

Adam had been wrong. Despite all the supernatural things Becky had seen, it was this world that scared her the most.

There was only one way out of the gangway, and that was back up the steps to the sidewalk. Or, if they wanted to surprise the folks who owned the two-flat, they could bust through their basement door, which had not just one but two padlocks on it. Becky and Adam decided to hold their breath and stay put.

"Just stay still, Becky," Adam whispered. "I'll protect you."

Finally, Elby got back into his car, mumbling something to the two men who had obviously been following Becky and Adam, then drove away. The other two men left without saying a word. Adam made Becky stay in the gangway while he crept up the steps. No one was around. The street had cleared out. He waved for Becky to join him, took her hand, and headed across the street.

"Where are we going?" Becky asked.

"We need to get somewhere where there are lots of people and..." Adam stopped.

"There! Over there!" The two men had had the same idea and had crossed the street but still spied Becky and Adam a block away.

Adam didn't waste any time. He grabbed Becky's hand, and they took off running. They whipped around the corner of Kenmore. The street was busy and Carlisle's Ice Cream Shop and Sundries was a fluorescent beacon of safety.

Cars were rolling past, people were talking and laughing, the businesses on the street were lit and filled. This was what they needed. Becky was aware of the smell of exhaust fumes from the traffic, and someone who had passed them smelled of jungle gardenia and cigarette smoke. Finally, they made it to Carlisle's and shoved their way inside. The entire counter was full of every kind of dame and gent, sipping chocolate sodas and sharing heaping bowls of ice cream. On the other side of the store, cigarettes, gum, stockings, peppermints, chocolate bars, aspirin, tonic water, plastic combs, and a host of other novelties were flying off the shelves. People were talking and waving, and it was almost as if this was the meeting place for everyone either before they had tossed back a few drinks or after.

"We'll be safe here," Adam said, panting.

"Yeah, if they don't see us. You duck inside there." Becky pointed to an empty phone booth. Adam did as she said while she stood close by. Quickly she scanned the room for any familiar faces. Not a one. But she smiled nonetheless.

"Hey, sister. Can I bum a ciggy?" she asked a plump brunette with thick, arched eyebrows who had just struck a match.

"Sure, doll. Say, is that your date?" The brunette jerked her chin at Adam, who was pretending to be on the phone while he looked over everyone's heads toward the door.

"Yes, he is," Becky said.

"That's one tall, cool drink of water. Does he got a brother?" she asked as she handed Becky a cigarette.

"No." Becky laughed.

"That's too bad." The girl struck another match and lit the tip for Becky. "If you ever get tired of climbing that tree, give me a shout. See ya."

The girl waved and scooted her plump form through the crowd of people and headed toward a back door. Becky watched as the door opened to what looked like the alley. She rapped on the glass of the phone booth and pointed it out to Adam.

Just as he stepped out, the men who had been following them appeared at the front door.

"Uh-oh," Adam said.

"Follow me. And keep your head down," Becky

said as she smiled happily, putting on a show as if she and Adam were just a couple of partiers like the rest of them.

When they made it to the door, Becky gave it a hard push. Just as Adam stood up straight to see where the two thugs might be, they shouted and pointed right at him. The crowd didn't budge for the men. Becky and Adam slipped out the door and into the alley. There was another speakeasy just a few feet away.

"They'll think we went in there. Let's go this way," Adam said, pulling Becky in the opposite direction.

They zigzagged and cut through alleys. They joined groups of partiers, inching their way along the sidewalk before slipping off alone. By the time Adam hailed a cab, Becky wasn't even sure she was in Savannah anymore.

"We have to have given them the slip," she said happily, scooting closer to Adam.

"Take the lady to the Old Brick Cemetery," Adam said. His eyes were narrow, and his lips were pinched together. "You cut through there like usual. No one will be likely to follow you through the boneyard."

"Okay," Becky said.

"You stay close to home. Don't go off on your own like you did today. I don't care if Fanny is your only option. You have someone with you at all times," Adam instructed.

"For how long?" Becky asked, her eyebrows pinched together.

"Indefinitely," Adam said.

"Adam White, if you think I'm going to be a prisoner in my own home, you're crazy. I'm not a child."

"Becky, just lie low for a while."

When the driver pulled up in front of the Old Brick Cemetery, Becky was in the middle of an argument with herself.

She kissed Adam on the cheek, climbed out, and slammed the door shut. As she walked deeper into the cemetery, the sound of the motor echoed over the desolate place until it finally disappeared in the distance. Becky said hello to her usual friends. Mr. Wilson walked a little ways with her, telling her about his grandson. A woman from the colonial days who had yet to offer Becky her name spied her and commented on the length of her skirt.

By the time Becky got home, she was exhausted and had ruined another pair of stockings. Part of her wanted to climb the trellis and avoid any human contact. But before she could, Fanny was on the doorstep.

"What on earth were you doing having lunch with a policeman in uniform in the middle of town without a chaperone?" Fanny asked.

"A chaperone? What good would a chaperone be if you're out with a policeman?" Becky looked at Fanny as if she'd suddenly sprouted a horn in the middle of her forehead.

"Don't get smart with me. Your mother is going to want to know," Fanny huffed, lifting her chin.

"How do you know about it?" Becky snapped.

"Mrs. Merriweather called. She spoke to Uncle Judge," Fanny replied coldly.

"My father told you what transpired in a private phone conversation between him and Mrs. Merriweather?" Becky stepped forward. "If he made such a breach of etiquette, I don't believe your Aunt Kitty will be very happy about that either."

Fanny swallowed. It was obvious that Judge hadn't told her what Mrs. Merriweather had called about. It was more likely that Fanny had either listened on the extension or eavesdropped outside Judge's office. Either was grounds for eviction.

"I'm just trying to spare your mother any more grief," Fanny said. "But if you think there is nothing to this story that is floating all around town, then I won't utter a word." She turned and went back inside.

Becky followed, restraining herself from giving Fanny a swift kick in her namesake.

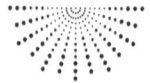

# CHAPTER SIXTEEN

"*B*ecky?" Judge called just as she closed the front door behind her.

"Yes, Daddy?"

"Could you come here a second? I'd like to talk to you." His voice was soft, deep, and serious.

Becky bit her bottom lip and shook her head. Fanny was probably loitering around the corner, drooling on herself like a dog waiting for a nice, juicy bone to tear into.

"Yes, Daddy?" she asked innocently, hoping he wouldn't pay any attention to her shredded stockings. "If this is about Mrs. Merriweather, I'm just going to tell you that it was an innocent lunch with an associate of yours, and there was nothing scandalous or vapor-inducing in the least. She's just a busybody who—"

"It isn't about that precisely," Judge said, clearing his throat. He was sitting behind his big oak desk, a thick cigar smoldering in the green glass ashtray next to his high-backed leather seat. He took a deep breath and looked at his daughter before he smiled.

"Looks like you've had a rip-roaring time."

"It was a lot of hustle and bustle. Let's put it that way," Becky replied before pulling up a chair in front of her father's desk. It was a simple chair shaped like a crescent moon with golden upholstery and dark wooden legs. When she sat down, she felt like a little girl again. This was one of her favorite spots, from which she'd often watched her father shuffle through his paperwork regarding the plantation: pay for his workers and land deeds and everything else that went with running a business as large as tobacco.

"I had to venture to the bank this afternoon. It must have been after Officer Ferris and you made a spectacle in front of Mrs. Merriweather." Judge winked. Becky rolled her eyes. "Now tell me, Rebecca, what does your dear old daddy like to do after I visit the bank?"

"You like to stroll over to the corner drugstore, buy a Hershey bar, and then go to the park at Courtland and Main. It was a beautiful day to sit in the park. I wish I could have joined you," Becky replied. "Tell me, how did that chocolate taste, since you didn't even think to share it with your one and only daughter?"

"Delicious. Now, as I was walking, I had a funny feeling I was being followed," Judge said, folding his hands in front of him.

Becky's heart lodged in her throat. "By who?"

"Well, at first, I wasn't sure. Sometimes you find a fella who needs a job and is hesitant to ask while tailing you because his pride gets in the way. Why, I've hired at least half a dozen men down on their luck and am proud to say the majority of them are still with us." Judge cleared his throat and scratched his chin thoughtfully.

"Sometimes it's nothing more than a hobo looking for a handout. Now, we've been blessed. Me especially. I've got your mother and you and all this land that is healthy and fertile. Yet it wasn't always so. I never forget where I came from and that sometimes a leg up is all a man needs. So I can spare a nickel or a dime, and I don't care what a fella does with it."

"But this was indeed different," Judge said. "I took a seat on my bench in the park and pretended not to be studying the landscape. Well, that very same fella you were having lunch with showed up at my side the instant I thought I was finally alone."

"Daddy, I didn't share a meal with him. There was something strange about that man. I hope I didn't cause any unnecessary rift between you and him," Becky said. She didn't dare tell him about the strange shadow that had been buzzing around Ferris. Her father would think she was losing her marbles.

Judge shook his head and pulled the corners of his lips down in an exaggerated frown. "The truth is I was shocked to see the man. We were newly acquainted. It wasn't as if he were kin or had some kind of history with me or your mama. So his request struck me as rather odd," Judge said.

"His request?"

"Why yes. After discussing the fine weather and the recent fight between Benny Leonard and Rocky Kansas, Officer Elby Ferris asked if he may call on you. Said he was smitten," Judge said before rolling his tongue against his cheek.

Becky stared at her father, her mouth hanging open.

"Careful or you'll catch flies," Judge teased.

"He wanted to call on me?" Becky felt queasy. "Daddy, I don't like this, not one bit."

"Well, I can assure you, my darling, that I was none too happy with it either. I asked him why he felt the need to approach me this way instead of formally coming to the house," Judge said. "He told me that he had known I was going to be in the city and thought now was as good a time as any to ask to pay you a visit."

"How did he know you were going to be downtown?" Becky asked.

"I asked the same question," Judge said. "He told me that you told him." Again, Becky's mouth fell open. "I knew he wasn't telling the truth, because I didn't tell you I was going into the city. I didn't know I was going until ten minutes before I was in the car."

"Daddy, what does this mean?"

"I'm not sure. But that isn't all he said."

"Oh goodness, I don't know if I want to hear any more," Becky gasped. An overwhelming urge to wash her hands and face overcame her as she shimmied a shiver off her shoulders.

"He said that he had nothing but the sincerest

intentions and that it was always good for a businessman like myself to have friends in the police department." Judge looked at Becky. "I didn't have the heart to tell him about Cousin Russell, who is the precinct captain on the south side of the city. I also didn't have the heart to tell him that I'm not the kind of man to be shaken down."

"Do you think that was all it was? A shakedown?" Becky swallowed hard. "You don't think he's really going to come calling on me. You won't force me to entertain him in the parlor or bring him Lucretia's sweet tea, will you?"

"I'm not your mother. Besides, I don't think your mama would want you to be a policeman's wife. It's a noble profession but a dangerous one. Especially in these times of ours." Judge shook his head.

"So where did things leave off with you two?" Becky asked.

"I informed him that I was almost positive that my one and only daughter had a fella and that I didn't interfere in things I knew nothing about. I advised him that in my opinion, there were a good many people who should stay quiet on things they know very little about. I am confident to say I do believe he got the message," Judge said. "However,

Becky, men like Elby, they need to be handled gently."

Becky wrinkled her face. She thought for sure guys like Elby Ferris needed to be handled with a pair of cement boots and swimming lessons off the pier.

"It's true. His pride is his most important thing. If you damage that in any way, you'll not just be dealing with a man with a bruised ego but a man with a badge and a gun and a bruised ego. Honey, do you understand what I mean?" Judge asked.

"I'm picking up what you're putting down, Daddy. I need to just be sweet as pie if I see the man again."

"I think that would be best. And let him down gently. In fact, you can blame it on your dear old pop if you want. Tell him I've forbidden you from going out alone with a man who I haven't specifically picked for you. That'll buy you some time." Judge winked.

That might have been a good idea except that Elby, or at least his men, had already seen her alone with Adam. And if they were the kind of people Becky suspected, they had already pieced together a scandalous escapade for today's activities. But she wasn't going to tell her daddy.

"All right, Daddy. Thank goodness Mama wasn't here to hear all this. I don't know how she'd be reacting knowing that a police officer was asking about me. The whole idea is almost comical," Becky said. "Oh, she'll be beside herself when she knows not only that Mrs. Merriweather saw my encounter with Officer Ferris but that then he tracked you down. Still, Daddy, how do you think he knew you were going into town today?"

"My guess is that there is more than one member of the Savannah police who monitors our quiet little road," Judge said.

"He's spying on us?"

"That's my only guess. He wouldn't be the first man to try such tactics. Look, there has been no reason for the man to react any other way than cordially."

Becky's stomach tightened again as she thought about him hunting her and Adam down. Sure, he had been polite to Judge Mackenzie, but he hadn't seemed to be all that copacetic when he was sending his goons after Adam and herself. For a second, she thought of telling her father about the incident but then thought better of it. This had something to do with Violet Darcy's death. There was no doubt about it. Maybe if she gave Elby what he was looking for, he'd leave her alone.

"And is Officer Ferris any different from Mrs. Merriweather?" Judge joked.

"Lord knows if that old biddy could set up camp across from our house, she would," Becky huffed.

"Well, don't you worry about her. I told her that my daughter was completely capable of taking care of herself and that I was sure any fella she joined for lunch was probably one of the finest gentlemen in all the South. I also told her she had her own daughter to tend to and that it might be wise that she do just that." Judge smiled at Becky's reaction.

"Daddy, you really are the bee's knees." She reclined in her seat and shook her head. "Well, I've had a long night. This has been too much. I might have a nightcap and take it to my room."

"Fix me one while you're up, sweetheart. That Mrs. Merriweather's husband must be up to the gills every night." Judge rubbed his temples.

"Don't let Mama hear you say that. Mrs. Merriweather's opinion is worth its weight in gold," Becky said as she poured bourbon into two short crystal tumblers with lots of ice.

"Don't you kid yourself about your mama, Rebecca. She only wants what's best for you. If she can help you along, that's all she wants to do. But mark my words, she wouldn't trade a single hair on your head for all the debutants in the South," Judge said, nodding as he took the glass from her hand. "Neither would I."

"Cheers, Daddy." They clinked glasses.

"See you in the morning," Judge said, leaning back in his chair and taking up his cigar.

Becky, on tiptoe so as to catch Fanny spying, hurried across the carpet, past the foyer, and to the stairs, where she walked dead down the center where the stairs didn't squeak or groan. When she realized the hallway was empty, she shook back her shoulders and figured it was out of fear that Fanny had decided to give Becky and her father some privacy.

But once inside her room after closing the door tightly, Becky walked in the dark to her vanity. She sat down, opened the top drawer, and took out the flask she'd found at Violet's. She sipped her bourbon and turned the thing over and over in her hands.

By the light of the moon outside, she looked at the bottom of the flask.

"Hmm... LB. Leonard Brennan. Elby Ferris." Her mind began to whir as if gears were shifting, stopping and starting. "Could it be? No."

Becky downed the last of her drink, got undressed in the dark and looked out her bedroom window for any suspicious activity out beyond the tobacco rows. She didn't see anything. But she couldn't shake the feeling there was something out there.

# CHAPTER SEVENTEEN

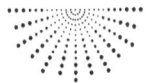

*T*he grandfather clock at the end of the hallway had just chimed three times when Becky's eyes popped open. She'd gone to bed hours earlier without talking to Fanny and after saying very little to her father. Her mind had been wrapped up in reliving the day's events. But now that she had been awakened by something, all of that came flooding back to her. Had she heard something downstairs? Had there been a gunshot? A window breaking? Had someone broken in?

Her body ignited as her heart began to race. Becky's most primal instincts kicked in. With her breath held deep in her chest, she didn't move a muscle but listened for the familiar creak of someone ascending the steps and heading toward her room. There was nothing. Her eyes focused on the door, the knob in particular. What if whoever— or whatever—was skulking around the house was already outside her door? She swallowed hard and squinted. There would be no need to open the door; it was already open. The thin black column of shadow darker than her room indicated the door was slightly ajar. Was someone out there in that shadow, watching her? Was it Leonard Brennan? Was it Elby Ferris, a member of Savannah's own police force?

Before she could pull the covers up over her face, a shuffle by her vanity made her yelp and sit bolt upright in the bed.

"Who is it?" she shouted.

The open window let in a gentle breeze that lifted the curtains slightly. The moon had repositioned itself and let a cool shaft of light inside Becky's room, illuminating the edge of her bed, her vanity, and the person sitting there.

"What? Fanny? Oh, jeez-o-pete. You nearly sent me to the sod buster." Becky fell back into her down pillows. "You aren't seriously putting on munitions at this hour. Please don't tell me you are so vain you doll up for bed. If you had someone *under* the bed, I could understand it, but why do I doubt you are that interesting?"

Becky waited for Fanny's gasp and a lecture on uttering such obscene scenarios. But nothing came. She looked at her cousin as she sat in front of the mirror, slowly combing her hair and studying her own reflection.

"Fanny? Don't tell me you are sleepwalking. If that ain't enough to upset the apple cart. When you are sleeping is when you are most pleasant," Becky huffed. "Now you're annoying me even when you are sawing logs. Fanny? Fanny, can you hear me?" Still no reply.

With a great sigh, Becky threw back the covers from her bed. The cool air instantly wrapped around her, raising goose bumps all over her arms and legs. The thin, silky material of her pajamas was not enough to keep her warm without the help of her thick bed cover.

"You are going to hear about this tomorrow." She huffed as she found her slippers with her bare feet in the dark. "I've heard stories that say if you startle a sleepwalker, they could seriously injure themselves. Do you have any idea how tempting this is for me, Miss Fanny Doshoffer? I swear, if this isn't the monkey's eyebrows. Of course you don't have any idea how much I'd like to let you run smack into a wall."

With her feet finally covered, Becky shuffled over to her cousin and put her hands gently on her shoulders to get her to her feet and guide her back to her bed.

"Come on, Cousin. You look fine. Fanny?" Becky said gently. "Fanny, we're going back to your bed now. Come on."

Still her cousin would not move from the vanity. Although she had stopped primping, she hadn't made any attempt to move. By this time, Becky was getting annoyed.

"Fanny, you are making this more and more difficult by the second. Now come on. Upsy-daisy." Becky managed to get Fanny to her feet. But when she did, her cousin whirled around, catching Becky off guard and causing her to fall over the foot of her bed onto her mattress.

"What in the world is wrong with you, girl?" Becky huffed as she pushed herself up. But before she could rise, Fanny was leaning over her.

"Why did he do it?" Fanny whispered. When Becky looked up, she saw the side of Fanny's face was a mass of bruises and swelling.

"Oh, Fanny! Oh my gosh! Who did this? Who did

this to you?" Becky tried to get up, but her cousin held her fast.

"Why did he do it?" Fanny sobbed.

"Who? Fanny, did you sneak out to see that policeman? Oh, Fanny, don't worry. I won't tell a soul. We'll make it right. Just tell me what happened," Becky whispered desperately.

"I picked the wrong one," Fanny muttered.

"That's okay, Fanny," Becky pleaded. "Just tell me what happened."

"He promised he wouldn't do it. But he did. Then he left me there. I was all alone. He left me there in the cold and on the ground all by myself." Fanny began to sob.

"Oh no, Fanny. Who did this? Who left you all alone? You've got to tell me. You've got to be strong and just tell me." Becky was frantic. She was starting to cry herself.

"I'll be... I loved him." Fanny's head rolled to the right.

"Loved him? Who? You give me a name, Fanny Doshoffer, and I swear Adam and the boys will do a number on him so fast he'll never think to raise his hand at anyone ever again. Just a name."

"You know!" Fanny hissed and leaned forward. Her eyes were swollen, bruised masses, streaming tears. She glared into Becky's face with black eyes squinting through the puffy skin.

It wasn't Fanny. Not at all.

Becky's own eyes filled with tears as she saw the real pain, the injuries that spread across the other woman's face and down her neck to her shoulders and arms. This wasn't Fanny. It was Violet, and she was using Fanny.

"Violet. You poor thing. Why didn't you come to me? Why didn't you come to Martha? We could have helped. I won't let him get away with this. I promise. Leonard will pay."

At those words, Fanny's face folded up into a mass of wrinkles as she squeezed her eyes shut and stretched her mouth open in a silent scream before leaving Fanny to collapse on the floor.

Becky quickly slid off the bed and to her cousin's side. Fanny was in an unresponsive heap. Just as Becky was about to scream for her father, a strange sound came from her cousin.

"Hwaaa. Hwaaa. Hwaaa," she snored.

Becky stood over her cousin. Her entire body was trembling at the sight she'd just seen. Never before had she been so scared. And here was her cousin on the floor, completely oblivious to what just happened, wheezing loud enough to wake the dead.

Becky let out a chuckle of relief while shaking her head. Part of her wanted to just throw a quilt over Fanny and leave her there. But that buzzing saw was not something Becky could fall asleep to. She'd have to get Fanny back to her own bed.

After snapping on the small light on the vanity Becky looked at Fanny's face. It had gone back to normal. She was a very pretty woman. It was too bad she had to open her mouth.

"Fanny? Fanny?" She gently shook her cousin, to no avail. "Fanny!"

"What? What? Where? What's going on? What time is it? Oh my Lord, what am I doing on the floor?" Fanny fussed as she groggily pushed herself up.

"That's what I want to know," Becky lied.

What else could she do? She certainly couldn't tell her the truth. Even if Fanny did believe her, how was that supposed to make her feel? Especially when Fanny had nothing but nasty things to say about poor Violet. Actually, the more Becky thought about it, the further she was leaning toward telling Fanny her body had been possessed by the girl at the speakeasy with the questionable reputation. She smirked at the thought.

"Oh dear." Fanny was finally on her feet. "I am sorry, Cousin Becky. This is very much unlike me."

"I do hope this doesn't become a habit, or I'll have to start locking my bedroom door," Becky harrumphed. "Or you'll have to start sleeping in the shed outside. You won't have to worry about night-time critters with the way you snore."

"What? I do not snore," Fanny hissed while wobbling sleepily toward the door. "Leave it to you and your poor taste to crack wise at this hour. Rebecca, you have no couth."

Becky rolled her eyes and followed Fanny to the door, closing it abruptly on her cousin's ample derriere, booting her into the hallway.

"No couth, Rebecca!" Fanny hollered before shutting herself up behind her own bedroom door.

Becky looked around her room. The flask she'd taken from Violet's apartment was standing upright in the center of the vanity table. After picking it up between her thumb and index finger, Becky looked it over. Nothing had changed. There was no new clue on it. There was no change in its composition. It was exactly the same as it had been when she'd laid it down just a few hours ago.

The image of Fanny's beaten face stuck with her. As she snapped off the light, she wondered what would make a girl stay with a man who could be so cruel. Once back in bed underneath the warm covers, Becky wondered how she would respond to Adam if he ever struck her. Would she forgive him if he begged her to? Would she make excuses for him? The thought that truly terrified her was the brutally honest answer: that she might forgive him if he did it once. And even if he did it again.

"He'll never do something like that, Becky. There's no use worrying over things that haven't happened," she scolded out loud into the dark room. The sound of her voice cutting into the quiet was startling. But as the curtains waved lazily on the light nighttime breeze, she didn't feel any consolation. And her eyes filled with tears as she wept for Violet, who had had the worst of luck, and maybe a little for herself for being blessed.

# CHAPTER EIGHTEEN

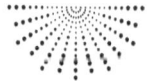

*B*ecky had taken the book Cecelia had given her to the Old Brick Cemetery to read. The white ceiling of clouds made it a perfect day to sit beneath her favorite tree dangling its pale green moss and read quietly with only the occasional roaming spirit to interrupt her with a friendly greeting or peculiar stare. As she finished the short chapter, she was relieved to discover that over time, these transferences dissipated. The last thing she wanted was to fine tune this skill and end up having some kind of flash of history in the outhouse at her favorite juke joint. As it turned out, the harsher the environment, the deeper the impression would be.

"I don't need to perfect this skill to know that

Leonard Brennan beat up Violet," she muttered, shutting the book.

As she stood up, feeling she'd spent enough time among the deceased, she stretched and took a good look around. What she saw made her wish she'd kept her nose in her book.

The entrance to the cemetery was on the opposite dirt road that ran parallel to the road that led to the Mackenzie plantation. Becky could see the crumbling, rusty gate from where she was. She also saw the police car that was idling there. Her heart pounded as she strained to see if the person behind the wheel had seen her. The driver's-side door opened, and a uniformed police officer stepped out. If he'd seen Becky, he thought nothing of it. But when he walked around and opened the passenger's side of the car, Becky gasped. She'd recognize that blond hair anywhere. Fanny had just gotten out of that police car.

"Oh Lord, please tell me she was arrested," Becky whispered as she hunched over and inched her way closer one tombstone at a time.

She was sure her cousin and her new friend hadn't seen her. Huddling behind the marker for Mr. Sloan Cunnings, Husband and Father, she peeked at the pair.

The police officer led Fanny to the front of his vehicle and quickly began flailing his arms, stomping his feet, running in one direction then stopping short to dash back again. Fanny laughed so loudly Becky could hear her from her hiding place. The officer continued his performance. From the looks of it, Becky assumed he was telling her about an arrest he made or some raid on a speakeasy. Either way, the whole scene made Becky furious. It obviously tickled Fanny, who laughed and clapped. Once he was finished with his strange display, the gallant officer offered Fanny his arm and escorted her to the passenger's side. With all the charm of a Southern gentleman, he held the door open as she got back inside. Then he hurried and got back in the driver's seat and, within seconds, had the red light spinning and the siren on.

"Oh, she is going to get an earful when she gets home," Becky said and started to walk to the Mackenzie house.

Lucretia had just come out on the porch to look for Becky and offered her a cold glass of lemonade. "What's the matter, girl? You look fit to be tied." Lucretia said after handing Becky the cold drink.

"Lucretia, is it a sin to want to slap someone who is kin?" Becky asked with a serious expression before peering at the housemaid over her glass of lemonade.

"*Slap* them? I think that might be one of those venial sins. I don't believe it would render one's soul permanently damned," Lucretia said. "Let me guess. You ain't hankering to slap yo father, and yo mama is out of town, so that leaves just one member of kin, correct?"

"You've a keen eye, Lucy."

Just then, they heard the sound of a motor pulling up the long driveway. Lucretia looked over Becky's shoulder.

"Goodness, that's a police car," Lucretia said.

"Go on in the house, Lucy. I'll handle this. Is my father still in the fields?" Becky asked, narrowing her eyes at the driver.

"Yes ma'am," Lucretia replied.

"Fine. Don't tell him about this. I will," Becky said just before Lucretia slipped back into the house.

Becky set her lemonade down and walked to the edge of the porch. Her stomach tightened as she watched the police car, the red globe still rolling on the roof. Thankfully they'd cut off the siren. The last thing she wanted was for the field workers to think there was a problem and come running.

The car stopped in front of the porch, and the

driver got out. Much to Becky's disappointment, it was Elby Ferris. He looked at her as if he was shocked to see her, but something in those feverish eyes made her think he knew exactly what he was doing.

"Good afternoon, Miss Becky," he said as he hurried to the passenger door and yanked it open for Fanny to get out.

"Is this a new service the police department is offering? Taxi service?" Becky jabbed. "You must be someone special to get to drive the police department's car all by yourself."

"Oh, Cousin Rebecca," Fanny gushed. "I just bumped into Officer Ferris while I was shopping in the city. There were some terrible boys down by the Cadillac Diner that were—"

"Let's just say they weren't acting very chivalrous," Elby interrupted.

"Officer Ferris put a stop to it and was kind enough to give me a ride home so as not to bother Moxley or Uncle Judge. Officer Ferris is good friends with Uncle Judge."

"Is that so?" Becky asked.

"Oh, now I'm sure your Daddy has told you about our little conversation the other day. That all still rings true, Miss Becky," Officer Ferris said with a devious look in his eyes. If lewd behavior could be conveyed through a glance, Elby Ferris would have been thrown in jail by his own captain.

"Really?" Becky replied.

"What conversation was that?" Fanny asked. Of course she did.

"Now don't you go worrying about it. Just a little talk among the men," Elby cooed.

"Is that all?" Fanny flirted, making Becky wrinkle her nose.

"Honest Abe." He held up his hand before taking her hand in his and kissing it. "Fanny, I do hope we can do this again sometime."

"I do too. Please come pay us a visit anytime," Fanny replied.

Becky rolled her eyes as Fanny made her way up the porch steps, swinging her hips like the pendulum in the grandfather clock. Becky took a step toward her and took hold of her wrist.

"I want to talk to you in a minute," Becky hissed.

"Why, Rebecca, you're embarrassing me," Fanny said before turning to catch Elby Ferris looking at her posterior, as she had assumed he would. "Goodbye, Officer." She waved.

"Uh, Miss Rebecca? May I have a word?" Elby asked.

With Fanny safely inside the house, Becky walked over to the edge of the porch.

"Come on down here. Don't make me hurt my neck looking up at you," he said.

Becky wasn't comfortable being all that close to Officer Ferris. He radiated heat, and the sickly look in his eyes made her uncomfortable.

"I think you and I should go out on the town together," he said, his words sounding oily and slick in Becky's ears.

"Oh, you see, my Daddy is rather particular about my dates, and he may not approve of me cavorting around with an officer of the law, especially when you lawmen have such difficult jobs. Why, how would it look if we were to be seen in company together one night and then you loading me and my friends in the back of a paddy wagon the next?" Becky thought her answer was rather smart. But Elby didn't.

"Oh, I don't think you'd ever have to worry about such a thing," he said. "Look, I do believe you have the wrong idea about me. I know that I come across rather bullish. I never was one for subtleties. But I'm afraid for you. I thought if we got to know one another, we could help each other."

"I don't know what I could possibly help you with," Becky honestly answered him.

"Sure you do. You knew Violet Darcy. You know her squeeze, Leonard Brennan." Elby said the name as if it caused pain in his mouth.

"I don't know him. I've only seen him, and when I did, he was with her. I don't think I ever said two words to the man," Becky stuttered. She hated that she sounded nervous. She didn't know why except that Elby was making her feel that way.

"Well, then why is he looking for you?" Elby asked innocently.

"He's *not* looking for me. Why would he be looking for me?" Becky started to talk very fast, but she was unable to stop herself. "Maybe he thinks I know something. Maybe you do too. But I can assure you I don't know anything. Just ask Fanny; she'll tell you. Not a thing. Did she tell you about Paris? I've been listening to her blather on and on about that for months now, and not a single word has stuck with me. That's what I mean. I don't know anything."

"You are cute," Elby said. The compliment made Becky shiver uncomfortably. He stuck out his hand for her to shake. "Just think about it. I could do a lot for you. I think we'd make a good team."

Becky accepted his hand because she had been raised to be polite. Suddenly it felt like she was holding tightly to a cactus. Elby squeezed, pulled Becky closer to him, and smiled kindly. She blinked as visions forced their way into her mind. They were awful pictures of Elby smiling. He smiled while he hurt people.

*Becky! Run!*

Becky focused as if she'd just woken up from a dream and stared at Elby before trying to pull her hand away from his. She'd heard a voice tell her to run. She looked over her shoulder, half expecting to see Fanny standing there, furious that she was still talking with Officer Ferris.

"Don't be like that. It hurts my feelings. Especially when I really am trying to keep you and your family safe. Leonard Brennan isn't just one dangerous man. He knows a lot of dangerous men," Elby said almost as if he was apologizing. "Some of them can even be your friends until the time suits them. It's really disappointing. You'd think they'd leave women and children alone, but the bad ones, the really bad ones like Brennan, they don't care."

With one final yank, Becky pulled her hand away and rubbed it tenderly. She looked down, expecting to see puncture wounds and scratches, but it wasn't even red. Still, she knew what she'd felt.

Without saying another word, Becky turned around and went back to the house. She didn't wait to see Elby leave. But she heard the sound of his car tires grinding over the pebbles and dirt of the driveway.

Once inside the house, she caught Fanny peeking out the window. "What do you think you're doing taking a ride from that man?" Becky snapped.

"Cousin Becky, what has gotten into you? I know for a fact that you'll jump in the front seat of any car going in any direction, so I would appreciate it if you didn't lecture me on who I allow to drive me home," Fanny replied, flipping her hair.

"Fanny, Officer Elby Ferris asked Daddy for permission to call on me," Becky said at the same time she put her hand to her stomach. The thought made her slightly nauseous.

"Is that so?" Fanny smirked. "Perhaps he wants to call on you so he can get to know me. Really, Rebecca. The color green doesn't suit you."

"Are you lit?" Becky snapped. "That's it, isn't it? Because only a rummy would pretend not to see through his act. He's using you to get at me."

"Rebecca, if there is one thing I've learned, it's

that it can be very beneficial to have friends on the police force," Fanny said as she pushed past Becky on her way to the stairs.

"You're doing this because you think he's interested in me, and you can't stand that," Becky hollered. "And I can't believe I'm even hollering about this. Fanny, there is something *wrong* with the guy."

"If he's calling on *you*, then no truer words were ever spoken," Fanny huffed. "All I did was accept a ride home. I was being harassed on the street, and he stepped in. I couldn't refuse his kindness and, quite frankly, I didn't want to. There isn't anything wrong with making friends. Let me rephrase that. There isn't anything wrong with making friends other than bouncers and hatcheck girls."

"You're going to learn your lesson the hard way," Becky said to Fanny's back.

She looked down at her hand, which was still tingling. Whose voice had she heard telling her to run? Why would anyone say that? She had been standing in front of her own house. What could happen to her? Still, the voice had been there. She knew she'd heard it.

# CHAPTER NINETEEN

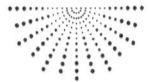

*B*ecky wondered if Fanny's transformation had been a message from Violet or a premonition of what was going to come. She threw back her second shot of bourbon since she had arrived at the river juke joint with her friend.

"Becky? What's eatin' you?" Martha asked.

"What?"

"I've been talking to you for ten minutes, and I don't think you've heard a word." Martha sipped her shot and took a drag from her cigarette. "You've been off in la-la land for days now. Come on. What gives?"

"It's Violet Darcy," Becky said.

"What about her?"

"I don't know. I'm not so sure that Leonard Brennan is the guy who killed her," Becky said, biting her lip.

"Whether he did or didn't doesn't matter. The cops will find the guy, and then he'll have a date with Old Sparky at Leavenworth. It doesn't concern you, honey," Martha soothed. "Come on. I can see a couple of lonely hearts over against the wall who are just waiting for you to look around so they can get in a dance."

Becky smiled.

"Now, that's better," Martha cooed. "Okay, honey, sit up straight. Cross your legs at your ankles. Shoulders back. Chin up. Now, look over to the lineup and set your sights on some poor joe. You know all those boys. Give one of them a wink, and let's start having a good time."

"You're right," Becky said. As much as she hated to admit it, it was Violet who was dead, not her. She was alive and well and in one of her favorite juke joints. The music was fine and the drinks were wet, and she was ready to let off a little steam.

Off in the corner was a new face. He was kind of soft all over, but he had the jimmy leg for the song that was playing. As soon as Becky caught his eye, he smirked and sauntered over.

"Care to dance?" he asked politely.

"I've been waiting for you to ask."

Becky hopped up and took his hand, and before she knew it, they were crammed snuggly into the crowd of dancers. Her partner was a fine dancer who not only could keep up with Becky but was quite funny with his expressions and quips.

When the song changed to something a little slower, he slipped his arm around Becky's waist and began to talk.

"I've seen you around town before," he said, that cute smirk still on his face.

"You have? Well, I hate to admit it, but I'm no stranger to the speakeasy." Becky chuckled. "You must have a favorite joint yourself to learn to dance like you do."

"Yeah, well, I enjoy a couple of spots. I think my favorite is behind a furniture store on Portage," the man said, staring down at Becky. He still had the smirk on his face, but it was no longer innocent. It was sinister, and the look in his eyes hardened.

Becky tried to push him away, but he held her tight.

"Relax, doll. I'm not gonna hurt you," he whispered. "We're going to finish this dance and maybe one or two more. Then you are going to tell me where you put that little item you stole from Violet's apartment."

"I don't know what you're talking about." Becky swallowed hard.

"Sure you do. And my boss knows you know. The truth is he doesn't want to hurt you or any of your friends. And I know you wouldn't want anything to happen to them either." He nuzzled in Becky's hair. "Just tell me where it is, and all of this goes away. Mr. Brennan will be forever in your debt."

Becky jerked her head back. "Did you say Mr. Brennan?"

The guy looked at her from under lazy eyelids. "Who else?"

"You mean you're not with Officer Elby Ferris?" Becky snapped.

The sound of the officer's name made the guy squeeze her even tighter.

"Please don't tell me you've given it to him," the man hissed.

Becky swallowed hard and shrugged. "I don't know what either of you are talking about. But both of you seem to think that I have something you both want. Maybe, if you tell me what it is and why it's so important, I can check to see if I accidentally picked it up."

"Okay. Why don't you and I go for a quick walk outside to get some air and talk this over." He slipped his hand over hers and squeezed it tightly.

Becky looked over her shoulder at Martha, but she was busy laughing with Teddy and Fanny. Adam hadn't shown up yet.

"Come on, doll. I'll make sure you make it back to your friends. We're just going to talk."

He pulled her through the crowd. A number of ladies called Becky by name and waved. Still more gents asked for a dance later.

Once outside, Becky looked around at the people sitting in the grass or on wooden crates with a dim candle between them and feared this would be her last speakeasy ever.

"Hey, Becky! Dance later?" came a squeaky voice from one of the small groups sitting on crates. It was a fellow Becky knew named Barney. He was a staple at this juke joint and a fine dancer.

"Of course, Barney," Becky replied quickly.

The man with the smirk gave her a tug and started to lead her in the direction of a couple of cars.

"Don't worry. You'll be able to dance with old Barney as soon as you tell me where it is," the man said as he tugged at the button on his collar and undid his tie.

"Look, I think you've got the wrong redhead. I knew Violet, and I knew her knuckle-dragging boyfriend Brennan. But I don't know anything about what you are looking for, because I stay away from trouble."

"Ha!" the man said. "What do you think? I fell off a turnip truck?"

"Everyone knows that Leonard Brennan had a heavy hand and a short temper. What he did to Violet was terrible, and she didn't deserve it. Everyone knows that too. And if you are an associate of his, chances are you don't have any problem roughing up the ladies too. Well, I ain't afraid of you," Becky snapped. "Now, I'm going back inside to join my friends."

With that, Becky yanked her arm away, turned, and headed straight for Barney. He wasn't the bodyguard type, but he would do in a pinch.

Before she could get three steps away, the man grabbed her by her arm and yanked her back.

"Let go of me!" she shouted.

"You make another peep, and I'll bust you right in the chops," the man hissed.

"That's no way to talk to a lady." Becky heard the voice coming from some shadows.

"Mind your own business, pal. This doesn't concern you," the man said, squeezing Becky's arm.

"Oh, I think it is my business."

The man stepped into view, but Becky didn't know whether she wanted to laugh or cry. It was Elby Ferris, out of uniform, in a dapper suit and two-toned shoes and a bow tie.

"What are you doing here?" The man obviously knew Elby. But Becky didn't think that was all that strange. Cops and robbers made strange bedfellows.

"Rebecca, are you all right?" Elby asked, his eyes glistening in the low lights and lanterns dangling from the trees.

"Uh, I think so," she replied. At the moment, she was sure Elby was the lesser of two evils. But this was a predicament she wanted no part of.

"Then why don't you go back inside," Elby said. "I'll have a nice talk with this gentleman, and I'm sure we'll come to a peaceful conclusion."

Becky didn't wait. She turned and ran back into the juke joint, pushed her way through the crowd of dancers, and flopped down next to Fanny, grabbing the first drink she laid eyes on.

"Hey, that was my bourbon," Fanny whined.

"I'm sure they won't run out," Becky huffed. She looked toward the door and waited to see one or the other of the faces she had left outside.

"What in the world happened to you?" Martha asked. "Don't tell me you lost your head over that guy. He was a good dancer but not all that easy on the eyes."

"What do you mean she lost her head?" Fanny interrupted. "Why, Rebecca, I thought you and Adam White were joined at the hip. He won't be very happy to hear about this."

"Pipe down," Martha scolded Fanny. "What's the matter, Beck?"

"Oh, nothing. That guy had me confused with someone else. You know how it is. All us redheads look alike." Becky chortled and grabbed another shot from the table and tossed it back.

Finally, her nerves began to relax, and her pounding heart started to slow. She kept looking toward the door, but no one was coming or going. It was as if everything was sort of stuck or frozen where it was. The only person she saw slinking through the crowd was Barney. He made his way up to the table and put out his hand.

"How about that dance?"

"Absolutely," Becky said.

She caught Fanny's grimace of disgust, as Barney was not a looker. His nose was thin and long, he wore round spectacles, and he really had no chin to speak of. It was as if he was perpetually tucking it down. But he was a good dancer and a real shot in the arm when Becky was out of sorts, like she was at the moment.

"You having trouble with those gents outside?" Barney asked as they danced.

"Oh, Barney, I feel like I'm having trouble with everybody these days." Becky sighed through a smile.

"Look, I know it's none of my business, but if you ever need money, I can help," Barney said in a hushed voice.

"What? What on earth would make you think that?" Becky asked, almost forgetting her dance steps.

"Well, I couldn't help but hear those two fellows outside. Once you were gone, one guy paid the other guy and said your tab was paid," Barney said innocently. "Like I said, I'm not trying to pry. But we all know that guys like that aren't always fair in their business dealings. I'd hate to have my favorite dance partner in any trouble."

"So, one guy paid the other one off? Said *my* tab

was paid?" Becky felt her blood start to boil. "It was a setup."

"Who says what now?" Barney stuttered.

"It was a setup. They followed me here, and that Officer Ferris orchestrated the whole thing so he could come to the rescue. Why, I'll bet that goon didn't even work for Brennan," Becky said through clenched teeth.

Part of her was relieved that she hadn't, in fact, been tracked down by one of Leonard Brennan's goons. But she had been tracked down by Officer Elby Ferris. As Barney led Becky around the dance floor, she caught a glimpse of her friends at the tiny table. She tripped herself and Barney and nearly caused a ten-couple-pile-up on the dance floor. Luckily, her partner was quick on his feet and rescued her from the embarrassment. But he couldn't rescue her from what was going on at the table. Officer Elby Ferris had wandered over and planted himself right next to Fanny.

Martha and Teddy were lit, having a great time and barely caring who joined the festivities. Fanny was talking to Elby, and as Becky watched her lips, she was sure the girl mentioned Paris at least three times in one sentence.

"Barney, would you mind walking me out for some air?" Becky asked.

"Not at all, Dollface." He offered her his arm.

Once outside, Becky took a long, deep breath. "So, tell me, Barney, how come you don't have a steady girl?"

Barney blushed and shook his head. "Well, you're with Adam White, ain't you. That'll answer that question," he flirted right back. "Speak of the devil."

Becky laughed and kissed Barney's cheek. "You're a good egg, Barney. Dance later?"

"You know it," he replied.

Becky saw Adam's silhouette approaching. They never arranged to meet at any of the speakeasies in town. Sometimes he showed up and sometimes he didn't. Becky rather liked their arrangement, which kept her missing him. But tonight she was thrilled to see him. But something was wrong with his gait. Becky waved, but he didn't wave back. As soon as he stepped into the pale circle of light, she saw why.

Adam had been beaten up.

# CHAPTER TWENTY

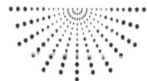

He stumbled into Becky's arms and nearly brought her down to the ground with him. He was drenched in sweat, and his body smelled of dirt and grass as well as the ink from the newspapers that never left him. As she struggled to keep him on his feet a little longer Becky could feel his body trembling.

"Barney, go inside and get Teddy!" Becky ordered.

Barney dashed off. The other folks outside the juke joint looked on curiously. A few of the gents hurried over to help.

"I'm all right," Adam said, forcing a smile that made him wince. "You should see the other guy."

"He'll be all right." Becky nodded. "Maybe if

someone could get some ice and soak it in some gin. That might do some good."

One of the patrons brought over a wooden crate for Adam to sit on, and he did so gratefully. Becky knelt in front of him, pulling a kerchief that smelled like lavender from her bosom and dabbing the bloody spot on his forehead.

"Good gravy. Did they take your money?" Becky asked.

"What?" Adam asked, jerking his head away from her touch. "That stings."

"Of course it stings. You're bleeding," she replied just as Teddy arrived with a glass of gin and some ice. Becky took the glass, dabbed her kerchief in it, and began to clean his face after handing the glass to Adam to drink.

"Jeez-o-pete." Teddy whistled. "You get the number on that train that hit you? Can we take you to a doctor?"

Adam looked up at Becky, who purposefully focused on cleaning his face. She felt Adam's chest expand as he took a deep breath then let it out slowly.

"No. Thanks." He let out another breath. "I'll be all right."

Now Becky looked Adam square in the eyes, her

right eyebrow bouncing at him. The left corner of his lip curled in as much of a smile as he could give without it smarting.

"What happened?" Becky asked.

"I was on my way here after having a bottle of suds with the guys after work." Adam licked his bottom lip, which was starting to swell. "I've been here what, a hundred times at least. Never any problems. Never any issues with anyone. But as I'm coming up the hill, I see three guys coming my way."

This had happened just after Elby Ferris made himself known. Shivers ran across her spine.

"Were they drunk?" Teddy asked.

"No. At least they didn't act drunk. They didn't sound drunk." Adam took another sip of gin. "The next thing I know, they're telling me I've crossed the wrong guy. And before I know it, I'm on the ground."

"Oh, my darling," Becky soothed. "It's all my fault. We need to get you out of here."

"I could use another drink," Adam said, lifting her chin with his index finger.

As much as Becky hated to admit it, in the golden light of just a few lanterns, with his hair all tousled and his skin slick with sweat, even with his bumps and bruises, Adam White looked good enough to eat.

"What happened here?" The voice was sharp and had a hint of too much alcohol around the edges.

"Our pal got jumped," Teddy offered. Becky turned around and saw Elby Ferris standing there. "If a big palooka like him can get jumped, that's a sad state of affairs we're in."

"Now that is a shame. Son, did you get a look at the guys who done this?" Elby asked, feigning concern.

"No," Adam replied.

"Well, you might say I have a few connections with the Savannah Police Department. I don't like to see this kind of thing happening to the citizens of this town. The Law of Prohibition must be upheld. But I don't see harm in anyone sneaking a toot now and again so long as it don't cause harm to themselves or others," Elby preached. "But this here kind of violence, well, it just turns my stomach."

Adam looked up at Elby, narrowing his eyes and clenching his fists. Becky felt the tension in Adam's wrists and quickly covered his hands with hers so Elby wouldn't see that Adam wasn't falling for his sermon.

"I think you ought to make a formal complaint with the police department. Why, if you come down there, I'll see to it personally that you are taken care of," Elby said, smiling broadly.

"No. It was just some guys who tied one on. I'm not injured badly," Adam said, pushing himself up so that he stood straight and looked down at Elby.

"Well, I am glad to hear that. If you change your mind, I'll make sure to leave my calling card at the front desk," Elby said before clearing his throat, adjusting his bow tie, and heading off.

"I think we better get you home," Becky said.

"That guy is a no-good liar," Adam hissed.

"You won't believe what's been happening since the last time I saw you," Becky rambled. "I've got so much to tell you that—"

"Whatever you have that belongs to Leonard Brennan, you need to give it back," Adam said. "Becky, these guys mean business. This is nothing compared to what they can do. Now what is it you are hiding?"

"What?"

"Becky, don't play me for a fool. If they think you have something, there has to be a reason for that. Let's face it, you do have a way of being in the wrong place at the wrong time."

"Well, doesn't that just put the cherry on top of this evening. You got yourself beat up for something that those goons are saying I have that I don't have. I don't know anything about it."

Becky hated to lie, but she knew that if any of her friends knew about the flask, they'd be pawns. As long as they didn't know anything, they were safe... at least in theory.

"You're sure you don't know what these guys are talking about? That guy that was just here, he's that cop from your father's poker game. The guy from the hooch lounge on Portage."

Becky nodded. "He's been popping up all over. Even spoke to Judge about me."

"Well, Becky, I think you are in a real pickle or a severe case of mistaken identity. Either way, you are going to have to lie low for a good while. Stay close to home and keep out of sight. If these hooligans think that you are out flapping your gums about one thing or another, they'll put a muzzle on you but good."

"I didn't do anything wrong. Why should I be a prisoner in my own home?" Becky felt the hair rising on the nape of her neck as her blood started to boil. "Since when do a bunch of street thugs tell me what to do?"

"Since they think you are the redhead they are looking for. And I hate to break it to you, Rebecca

Madeline Mackenzie, but there aren't that many redheads in Savannah. The pool of suspects is pretty small."

Becky looked up at Adam and put her hands on her hips.

"Promise me you'll tone it down just a little until this blows over?" Adam asked.

"I'm not promising anything," Becky replied defiantly.

Adam chuckled, leaned down, and gently placed his lips on hers. Oh, she was so mad at him. Even his bruised, cut lips were silky soft, and his sweat smelled clean, and his big muscles stretched the fabric of his clothes. Oh, how Becky hated him at this moment for making her love him. She rose on her tiptoes to make the kiss last just a few seconds longer.

Martha and Fanny arguing with one another snapped the two lovers out of it.

"I'm just saying how do you know you were in Paris, France, and not in Paris, of the Republic of Texas. You know, they speak so strangely down there, you might have been speaking Spanish and don't even know it."

"Well, I can see why you and Rebecca are such good friends," Fanny huffed.

"I'm just asking questions, that's all. Don't get sore. Speaking of sore, Adam! You look like John Merrick!" Martha slurred.

"Oh, he doesn't look that bad." Becky pinched her girlfriend's arm.

"Well, he doesn't look that good," Martha replied.

"Oh, Adam. Does it hurt?" Fanny gasped while batting her eyelashes.

Finally, Teddy arrived with the car, and everyone piled in. It was a long drive with Martha and Fanny still squawking and Teddy adding a wisecrack every couple of seconds. But Becky sat on her knees in order to hold Adam's head against her bosom and stroke his hair. She thought about his request to stay close to home and out of sight for a while. She would consider it. After all, what would she really be missing?

# CHAPTER TWENTY-ONE

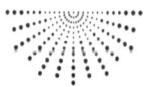

"*F*anny, in all this time you've been in Savannah, am I supposed to believe you haven't found one beau that strikes your fancy who can take you out on the town so you can leave me be?" Becky whined as she slipped on a new pair of stockings.

"If I was interested in meeting just anyone, well, of course there are oodles of gents to pick from," Fanny said while patting her hair into place as if a single strand dared lie awkwardly across her brow. "But after meeting the eligible bachelors in Paris, the men here in the States are, well, just a little rough around the edges."

"That's the best part about them," Becky snapped.

"My goodness, Rebecca, don't you ever think

before you speak? If anyone other than me heard you speak so crudely, they'd think…"

"They'd think what?" Becky's right eyebrow arched.

"They'd think you were a trollop. There. I said it. Are you quite happy now?" Fanny put her hand on her hip and stared at Becky from her bedroom door. "And I just don't think your poor mother needs something else to worry about while she's tending to your kin."

"Well, I'm going to Teddy's, and I suggest you stay here and wait for Mama's call. Then you can have a nice long chat and tell her all about me," Becky snapped as she grabbed the new two-tone T-strap shoes she'd placed on the bed and scooted past Fanny out her bedroom door.

"You know I'm only looking out for your well-being. You need someone around who has seen part of the world. And your mama said that I was to accompany you on any excursions out of this house that you might take," Fanny said, grabbing the clutch she'd conveniently left in the foyer.

Once on the porch, Becky hopped on one foot as she slipped on her right shoe and then the left. "Fine. You can come." Becky let her arms flop at her sides. "I swear, if anyone needs a man, it is you."

"There you go again. The language that comes out of your mouth is no better than a drunken sailor's," Fanny huffed.

"That's the ticket! A sailor. That's what you need. You know, those fellas know how to treat a lady, especially when they've been out at sea for a couple of months. Oh, Fanny, I am so glad you gave me that idea." Becky clapped as she stomped in the direction of the Rockdale home. "There's nothing more handsome than a man in uniform."

Becky chuckled as she looked off to the west, where the sun had dipped deeply behind the horizon, dragging a purple tail across the sky before it was all consumed in the black night. Fanny, who was wearing higher heels and wasn't as familiar with the path, wobbled back and forth as she followed Becky, groaning and criticizing the whole way.

It had broken Becky's heart when she'd thought someone had roughed Fanny up. Annoying as she was, Becky cared for her as a family member and just as a person. Becky was almost angry with herself for having such a stripe of compassion when she knew that Fanny hadn't the slightest concern for her. It seemed the only time Fanny was interested in Becky was when she was going out to paint the town red or when some juicy piece of gossip that had

Becky's name on it had floated to the surface. But Becky didn't give a fig about what Fanny was up to during the day or night. She was sure none of it was all that interesting.

*"That's what makes you special. Along with a laundry list of other things."* Becky heard her daddy's voice as clear as day, as if he were right there reading her thoughts. It was comforting, but not loud enough to drown out Fanny's sermon going on ten paces behind her.

"Can you just shut your piehole?" Becky snapped.

A gasp was Fanny's reply.

"Halt! Who goes there?" Teddy shouted before Becky could even see the place.

She heard the heavy, lazy sound of a trumpet coming from the Victrola and a woman singing about her baby leaving at night.

"'Tis I, Rebecca, and my trusty steed, Fanny!" Becky shouted.

"Very funny." Fanny snorted.

"Welcome! I'll lower the drawbridge!" Teddy laughed as he bounded down the front porch steps to greet his guests. "So, what's shakin'?"

"Is that who I think it is?" Martha shouted from the front door. "Becky, I swear you can hear ice melting in a mint julep a mile away."

"I don't know if you are aware that you are in the presence of a real cuddler. I couldn't leave you alone and let your reputation be ruined." Becky elbowed Teddy playfully in the gut.

"What happened to you, Becky? I used to be able to trust you with all my secrets," he teased. "Hello, Miss Fanny. You are looking as lovely as ever." Teddy took her hand in his and kissed it sweetly.

"Why, Teddy, I do believe you get more and more charming every time I see you," Fanny purred as she slowly pulled her hand away and slinked toward the porch. "Do you have a cold drink for me?"

"Of course I do." He offered her his arm, which she happily accepted.

Becky rolled her eyes at Martha, who covered her mouth as she giggled before handing Becky the mint julep that had been intended for Teddy. The girls sat down on the porch swing together and began taking turns chatting while alternately sipping their drinks.

"Come with me, Miss Fanny. Looks like we'll have to mix our own drinks," Teddy said, leading Fanny into the house.

"Are you sure you want to leave those two alone in there?" Becky asked.

"After all the time we've spent together, if she

wanted him, she probably would have sunk her claws in him by now. She's a real tomato," Martha said then took a sip of her mint julep. "Besides, it isn't my Teddy she's sharpening those claws for."

"Is that so?" Becky took a drink of her mint julep and looked out to the front yard. The Rockdales had half a dozen tractors, a fountain, a white picket fence, and at least twenty honeysuckle bushes scattered all over their front yard. It was several acres long, just like the Mackenzies' front yard, and perfect for daydreaming and planning and watching the sky get darker and darker.

"I swear she drools like an old hound dog when your Adam comes around. Can we expect to see the big brute tonight? Or maybe he'll be playing cards with your daddy," Martha said. "I think that's wonderful that Uncle Judge is getting to know him. Maybe that will soften Aunt Kitty up a bit."

"I don't know about that," Becky said. "If he isn't wrapped up in a Confederate flag and holding a great big Georgia peach, I'm not sure what it will take to get her to soften up."

The ladies chatted for a while longer until Teddy and Fanny returned with full glasses of their own.

"Martha, I must say that your Theodore was the most adorable baby. I just couldn't look away from those pictures in the parlor. If your children take after his side of the family, they'll be the most adorable little nippers ever," Fanny said.

"Is she drunk already?" Martha whispered as Fanny playfully messed up Teddy's hair, making him smile all the more.

"Nope." Becky said before taking a sip of her drink.

As the evening continued, everyone was having a swell time, cutting up, listening to the music, and sipping their cocktails. The light breeze dragged long carpets of clouds across the sky. The moon was bright again as it outshined the millions of stars around it.

"What's that?" Fanny pointed off in the distance.

"Teddy, are you expecting more company?" Martha asked. "Looks like someone coming down the drive."

"I wasn't expecting anyone. Maybe it's Adam. I ran into him a couple of days ago, demanding a chance to win some of my money back. You know that Northerner took home four dollars? Three of it was mine," Teddy huffed. "'Tain't fair for a man from north of the Mason-Dixon Line to swindle a Southern gentleman's money."

"You're just no good at poker." Becky chuckled,

feeling a slight buzz in her head as she watched Fanny stand up, smooth out her dress, and strike a pose against the railing. It was like a hen ringing the dinner bell for a pack of foxes. "I don't think that's Adam's jalopy. Doesn't sound like it."

"You can tell from this far off?" Fanny folded her arms, pushing up her ample bosom.

"I can. And that is not Adam's car." Becky looked down the long dirt road that merged into the Rockdale driveway and knew it wasn't Adam's car. Part of her was disappointed, but another part of her was glad it wasn't him. After what Martha had said, Becky didn't care to see Fanny throwing herself at him at every turn.

As the flivver got closer, there was no mistaking who was driving.

"Well, I'll be a monkey's uncle. That's Stephen," Teddy said. "We haven't seen him since the big brawl."

Becky's cheeks turned beet red as she rolled her eyes and took a long sip from her drink. She was going to need a refill immediately.

"I'm sure he's terribly embarrassed," Martha said. "It was the heat of the night. So much went on. He wasn't thinking straight."

"You can't blame a fella who acts the fool for a

woman, Rebecca. He was only thinking of you. How many men would go out on a limb like that for a lady? Not many in this day and age. That says something about his character that is quite admirable," Fanny said.

Becky thought she sounded like a political campaign manager.

"What did he do wrong? Just have a tussle. Why, I remember a terrible fight I got into over a girl. It lasted about as long as the White-versus-Penbroke bout. But I was willing to fight to the death for that girl," Teddy said, clicking his tongue and winking.

"What girl was that?" Martha squawked.

"That was Abigale Householder in my third-grade class. Boy, she was something." Teddy whistled, making all the girls laugh. "I knew I'd never find another girl like her. She had a lisp and a lazy eye that I was just ducky over."

Even Fanny was doubled over from laughing when Stephen's car came to a complete stop. Becky had lost her nervousness at Teddy's tale of unrequited love and even smiled at Stephen as he got out of the car.

"I stopped by your house, Miss Mackenzie, and your daddy was kind enough to tell me where to find you," Stephen said before giving Teddy a hearty handshake and Martha and Fanny each a peck on the cheek. He didn't dare approach Becky that way.

"Hello, Stephen. Would you like a mint julep? I was just about to refresh my glass. Anyone else while I'm up?" Becky asked as she stood up from the swing.

"Oh, please, allow me. This is my humble domicile. I'll handle the drinks. Martha, would you mind giving me a hand?" Teddy asked, quickly taking Becky's silver tumbler and hurrying inside.

"Of course. Fanny, would you mind helping me change the record?" Martha asked, jerking her head toward the front door.

"Changing a record is simple, Martha. You just pull up the needle, take off the record, replace it, and then replace the needle." Fanny pinched her eyebrows together as if Martha had asked her to wear a squid on her head.

"Then can you help me replace the needle, please?" Martha's eyes bounced from Stephen to Becky and back to Fanny while she jerked her head toward the front door.

Fanny pursed her lips and shook her head as she mumbled to herself about the Victrola before Martha grabbed her by the hand and whispered in her ear that Becky and Stephen needed a moment alone.

"They're quite subtle, aren't they?" Becky huffed.

"I'll say," Stephen said and stepped cautiously up to Becky. "I'm sorry for the way I behaved the other night."

"It was embarrassing. Both of you boys rolling around like pigs in slop," Becky huffed. "Fanny might like that kind of display by two gents, but I do not."

"You're right. But Becky, it still doesn't change how I feel about you. I know what you'll say. Adam is your beau," Stephen replied as he shifted from one foot to the other. "But I'm a Southerner. That we have in common, and when it comes down to brass tacks, it's the things we have in common that keep us together. You'll see."

"Are you saying Adam doesn't feel that way simply because he's a Northerner? My goodness, have you been talking to my mama?" Becky folded her arms.

"I'm saying that we have a common root. Plain and simple. And it runs deep. We understand each other in ways that people from the North just don't understand. It don't make them bad. It just makes them Northerners." Stephen smiled. "I think deep down, you know I'm right. But if you don't, I'll wait."

"Stephen Penbroke, you are a real dilly," Becky huffed.

"Do you forgive this Southern boy for his poor behavior?" Stephen asked before getting down on one knee and taking Becky's hand in his. "I would be forever in your debt, Miss Rebecca Mackenzie, if you'd find it in your heart to relieve me of this terrible burden of guilt."

"Oh, a real dilly." Becky rolled her eyes while trying not to laugh.

Stephen saw he'd cracked her shell and smiled in a very charming way that made his eyes sparkle and his cheeks lift high and round.

"Is that a yes?" He got to his feet and stood dangerously close to Becky, who stood her ground defiantly but ended up being somewhat vexed by Stephen's sweet cologne and the feel of his warm hands still holding hers.

"No more fighting?" Becky asked.

"No more fighting. I'd hate to hurt Adam. I really don't have anything against the man," Stephen said.

Becky was sure she was picking up on some undertone of sarcasm.

"He is a good egg," Becky argued.

"I agree. And I can't blame him for clinging to the prettiest skirt to ever set foot in a speakeasy. If I were in his shoes, well, I think you know what I'd do." Stephen winked.

"Stephen, you are full of applesauce. Everything you're saying is just a bunch of static. But I do accept your apology. What Adam plans to do is another story. But I'll put in a good word for you. Maybe he'll leave you to be my umbrella any time he can't make it."

"Umbrella? I'm not just a stand-in. I plant myself. I don't plan on going anywhere, no matter what anyone says." Stephen tugged at his collar, smoothed out his tie, and gently flipped a couple of strands of Becky's curls behind her shoulder.

His fingers grazing her neck sent shivers up her spine. She avoided his eyes for fear of what she might see in them. Maybe desire. Maybe love. Maybe she'd see herself in them, and that was just too much after all she'd seen. Part of her wanted to tell Stephen about Fanny's transformation, if for no other reason than to change the subject. But what would Stephen think of that?

Before she could open her mouth, the rest of the gang returned from the kitchen.

"Well, folks, we've got a serious problem," Teddy said as he stepped through the front door. "Looks like we are out of bourbon and ice."

Becky gasped. "What? How can that be? Teddy, I'm shocked to my very foundation! Martha? Martha, where are you? I think I'm going to lose my head."

"Very funny," Teddy huffed. "Keep your blouse on. I know where I can get some lickety-split. Stephen, old chum. Can I borrow your flivver?"

"I'll go with you, Theodore. I just love riding in an open-topped car in the evening time," Fanny cooed.

"I'll do you one better, Teddy. I know where to get the bourbon and the ice. You are the host. Let me make the call for reinforcements. I'll be back in a jiffy," Stephen said while twirling his keys on his finger. "Miss Fanny, you are more than welcome to accompany me."

"I think I'll do just that." Fanny giggled as she hurried to the car.

Within seconds, the car engine had choked to life. Stephen and Fanny waved and honked the horn as they turned the vehicle around and drove back down the long dirt drive, leaving a dark plume of dust in their wake.

"Why do I get the feeling those two going off together was not the best idea?" Becky said. "Sort of like a match and gasoline."

"Oh, those two have their eyes wide open," Martha replied. "Wide open."

"What do you mean?" Becky asked.

"Nothing," Teddy interrupted. "Martha likes to see shadows where there is nothing. Don't stir up any trouble, my darling, especially when Stephen is trying so gallantly to make amends."

"You're all wet," Martha said. "I'm just saying those two are cut from the same cloth. It wouldn't surprise me if they were scheming and plotting some kind of dance number. I don't know what it could be or who it would be directed toward, but I can guess."

"Not after Adam almost killed him. My goodness, if Daddy hadn't interrupted them, Stephen would have been cooled. Adam's not the kind of mug to go off the rails, but he was in a serious pickle when Stephen charged him. What was he supposed to do?" Becky felt she was babbling. "To be honest, I'd like to just forget the whole thing happened. Can we do that?"

Teddy and Martha looked at each other and chuckled. Becky flopped down onto the wicker chair with the high back, folded her arms, crossed her right leg over her left, and pouted. She was sure if two macs as dapper as Adam and Stephen were rolling around in the dirt over Fanny, her cousin would be to the moon about it, and even the fellas would be proud of their behavior over her. But it made Becky terribly uncomfortable, and she wished Fanny and Stephen would just stay out together and forget to return.

Unfortunately, only half of her wish came true. Stephen came back. But Fanny was missing. Kidnapped was the more appropriate word.

# CHAPTER TWENTY-TWO

*T*he flivver was moving slowly as it made its way back up the driveway after being gone for more than an hour. Becky, finally tired of waiting for Fanny and Stephen to return, had gone back to her house, where she'd grabbed a couple bottles of champagne and, before leaving, snagged the silver flask with the inscription on the bottom. She couldn't say why she'd brought it back with her. It was in her hand as she walked back across the yard.

"What in the world has taken you so long? My mouth is like the Sahara Desert," Martha called out to the car. "Oh, I get it. They're lit. Look at how the car is weaving and how slowly he's driving. Isn't that the living end? Those two mooks went out on the town without us."

Becky squinted then shook her head. "I don't think they're drunk, Martha. I don't see Fanny at all." She dashed down the porch steps.

"Maybe she's in the rumble seat passed out?" Martha added, trying to present a logical answer but realizing too late there was none. Fanny wasn't in the car. And Stephen looked like he'd gone toe to toe with a locomotive.

"What happened to you?" Becky cried. "Martha, get some ice and iodine! Teddy, help me get him out of the car!"

Martha's eyes nearly popped out of her skull before she nodded and dashed back into the Rockdale home to get what Becky had asked for. Teddy, always the gentleman, pushed Becky aside and practically carried Stephen to the swing under the porch light.

Stephen was an awful mess. His right eye hosted a shiner that nearly closed his whole eye. His lip was bleeding and puffy at the corner. His clothes, which had been so dapper just a short while ago, were now covered in grime except in the front, where his knees were now poking through the fabric. They were bleeding too. His hands were black and trembling around the steering wheel.

"Did you get a look at the guy who did this?" Teddy asked as Becky poured Stephen a full glass of champagne.

"Where is Fanny?" she asked as she handed him the glass.

He tossed it back and winced, looking up at Becky as if she just handed him a glass of castor oil.

"No. We got jumped from behind," Stephen said. "The only thing I saw were a couple of fists and size-eleven spats."

"You've got a goose egg on the back of your head," Teddy said.

"Stephen, where is Fanny?" Becky asked again.

Inside her chest, her heart was racing. Every second that she didn't know what had happened to her cousin was that much more time Fanny could be in trouble. Didn't anyone else realize that? Fanny hadn't a lick of street smarts. She wouldn't know how to fight back if her life depended on it. All she knew was that this kind of thing never happened in Paris. The idea of scratching or kicking or biting anyone to get away would be preposterous to her. Who would behave in such a way? Except maybe Cousin

Rebecca. Becky could hear Fanny uttering those words as if she were sitting on the porch right next to her.

Martha finally arrived with a couple of rags, a dishcloth filled with the last of the ice, and a bottle of iodine.

"Fanny and I were walking to the drugstore. You know that joint around the corner that sells the booze out the back if you've got the right password?" Stephen said.

Becky knew the place well. Her friend Mickey O'Donnell sometimes worked the door there. It was nothing more than a basement with crates of booze stacked up in rows of bourbon, rye, gin, and all the rest. There were three small tables if you wanted to enjoy a snort on the premises, but most people took it to go. There were only a few scratches on the brick wall in the alley to let anyone know the place was there. But that was how it was with most speakeasies. Becky was sure the coppers knew all about it but had been bought off to look the other way.

The problem with small places like that was that unlike clubs like Willie's that wanted people to have a good time and spend their money, this kind of literal hole in the wall was off the radar. It was in a kind of no-man's land. Even the gang laws didn't apply, and no one ever saw anything.

"Yeah, I know that place," Teddy said, nodding and looking at Martha as she dabbed the scratches on Stephen's head.

"Nothing looked different. I didn't get a cold draft when I went to the door." Stephen shook his head. "I knocked and gave the guy the password. Fanny was telling me about something she did in Paris. The next thing I know, my legs gave out. Before I could get back to my feet, I was being pummeled."

"How many were there?" Martha asked.

"I don't know. I think three, maybe four guys," Stephen replied.

"Great balls of fire! Where is Fanny?" Becky shouted.

Stephen looked up at her with tears in his swollen eyes.

"They took her. And they gave me this note. They knew your name, Becky. They told me to get this to you. Becky, what is this all about?" Stephen handed Becky a crumpled piece of paper.

She slowly took it from him as if she was handling a viper. When she opened the paper, the words glared at her like a wolf that was circling and watching her from the shadows, its teeth bared.

"What does it say?" Martha asked.

"It's Violet's old address," Becky said, her voice shaking. "The basement."

"That's a ritzy part of town. Everybody has deep pockets, and not just for the cash. There are some real tough cookies around that neck of the woods," Teddy said. "My father cuts through that neighborhood to get to the docks. You can't go there, Becky. I'm calling the police."

"If you call the police, Fanny will end up like Violet," Becky gasped. "No. You can't call the police. My gut tells me the police won't help. Not this time. Any other time and I know they would, but not this time. I've got to go, and I've got to go alone."

"Becky, honey, how are you going to get there when you don't drive?" Martha asked sadly. "I guess you're stuck with us. You didn't think we'd let you face these people alone, did you?"

"Wait a minute." Stephen pushed Martha's hand away from his face. "We aren't really talking like we're going to go busting in on some gangsters like the Feds, are we?"

"They have Fanny. What would you suggest?" Becky asked.

"First, I think we need to know what's going on. These goons know you, Becky. *Did* you steal something from them? What kind of a fool thing was that to do?" Stephen barked as he pushed himself up from the swing.

Becky took a deep breath and looked at her friends. "It was after Violet was killed. I was down in that neck of the woods where she was found and just did a little snooping."

"Becky. My Lord, gal, you know who she ran with. Why would you do that? What did you expect to find?" Teddy asked, running both his hands over his hair.

Becky thought from his expression that he looked almost impressed, like maybe this was one of those stunts to top them all that he'd be telling his pals about over beers the next time the temperature climbed above ninety. That is, if they lived through this.

Becky swallowed hard. "I didn't find anything. Not until Leonard Brennan and his goons showed up. When I hid on the fire escape, I—"

"You hid on the fire escape? Good gravy!" Stephen gasped.

Becky bit her lip. "I hid on the fire escape and accidentally kicked over a couple of pots she had stacked out there. I found this." Becky pulled the silver flask from her pocket. "It's inscribed with Leonard Brennan's initials and Violet's. At least, I think that's whose initials they are. They might stand for Elby Ferris."

"Who is Elby Ferris?" Martha asked.

"That's *Police Officer* Elby Ferris," Becky replied. "Remember the guy at that speakeasy when we were running from Leonard? The creepy guy with the glassy eyes and—"

"And the blonde who went running from the room they were in together?" Martha replied. "He was a cop? Now I understand why you don't want to call them."

"He saw me at Violet's. I don't know how. But you know how cops are. They have eyes and ears everywhere," Becky said. "Look, I'd love to stroll down memory lane with all of you, but the more time we waste putting all the pieces in place, the less chance we have to save Fanny. Martha, would you drive me?"

"Saddle up," Martha said, standing and stretching her hand out for Teddy's car keys.

"What? Absolutely not!" Teddy shouted.

"Wait, Teddy. Martha might have just the perfect idea," Becky said. "No one will think twice about two tomatoes going into this place. We're harmless and innocent and just happy to give back this dirty old flask and take Fanny. If we come with muscle, well, that might send the message we want a rumble. I don't know about y'all, but I don't want a rumble."

"Becky has a point. So, Martha, my dear, here are the keys. Stephen, are you feeling all right to fold yourself up in the back seat?" Teddy asked.

"What?" Becky snapped.

"I'm feeling just ducky. In fact, I think a drive all the way across town, crouched down in the back seat, is just what the doctor ordered," Stephen said, dabbing his lip, content that the blood had stopped for now.

"You two are impossible. Whatever you want to do, do it quick. Fanny is relying on us. She must be terrified," Becky said as she and Martha ran to the barn where Teddy kept his car.

Within minutes, the engine was chugging, and the lights were cutting through the darkness. Martha was behind the wheel with Becky next to her, and the boys were down on the floorboard of the back-seat. The driving skills of Miss Martha Bourdeaux were the kind of skills drivers in the Indy 500 would kill for. She talked almost as fast as she drove, every once in a while taking her eyes off the road to look at Becky or her hands off the wheel to make some grand gesture. Becky was white knuckled the entire way into the city.

Suddenly, Becky was seized by an invisible force. Something was in the car with her and her friends. Something angry.

# CHAPTER TWENTY-THREE

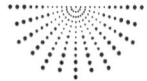

*I*t was as if Becky had suddenly come down with a fever. Her body ignited. Her mouth went bone dry, and her eyes began to water. Martha was talking about something, her hands were flailing, and she was shifting the gears in such a way that the car jerked and groaned but refused to stall.

"What did you say?" Becky asked. Her voice sounded to her as if she had stuck her fingers in her ears.

When Martha replied, she sounded like she was underwater. Becky looked down at the flask, and instead of seeing her own bright-red hair in the reflection, she saw black hair. It wasn't her. The face was distorted by thin etched lines, but Becky was sure it wasn't her own face she was staring at.

Carefully, she looked at Martha. Did Martha see Becky, or did she see the dark-haired reflection that could only have been Violet? She waited for her friend to stop speaking and scream in bloody horror, but Martha did no such thing. Instead, she just kept talking.

Becky looked at the flask and hoped the chills would pass and that maybe, just maybe, she was hallucinating due to the stress of Fanny being kidnapped. But as she leaned closer and pulled the silver flask up to her face, she was so close her breath made a circle of steam. Before it could fade away in the nighttime air, the initials LB appeared.

"Yes, Violet. I know. Leonard Brennan," Becky whispered.

Within seconds, the flask became scalding hot, and Becky dropped it to the floor with a yelp.

"What's the matter with you?" Martha asked.

"Just butterfingers, I guess. Nerves," Becky replied, suddenly feeling like herself again.

In fact, with her head free of fever, she had to ask herself why she was letting her friends walk into this trap. They had nothing to do with this, and they couldn't pay the price no matter what. She had to send them off in another direction, and as Martha whipped around the corner, she saw the perfect detour on her map.

"Hey, pull up there. I need some cigarettes." Becky pointed to Carlisle's Ice Cream Shop and Sundries.

"Cigarettes at a time like this?" Martha squawked.

"What do you mean? Now is the perfect time. This could be my last puff. You aren't going to deprive me of that, are you?" Becky tried to joke.

"Oh, Becky, don't say such things. Of course this won't be your last puff," Martha said. "How are you boys back there? Need anything from Carlisle's?"

"Maybe a back brace for when we get out of this pickle. I'm going to be a hunchback for sure," Teddy replied, barely poking his head up.

"How about you, Stephen?" Martha teased.

"I wish I would have made out my last will and testament," he grumbled.

"That makes two of us," Becky replied. "You wait right here. I'll be back."

She hopped out of the car, slamming the door behind her. She dashed into the store, which was as crowded as it had been when she and Adam had slipped in while trying to elude Elby Ferris's hench-men. Squeezing through the people lined up three deep against the counter, Becky finally managed to get to the back door. She looked around to make sure none of her entourage was following her. When she saw the coast was all clear, she dashed to the door, pushed it open, and fled down the alley in the direction of Violet's apartment.

As she hustled down the sidewalk, weaving in and out of the thin foot traffic, she hoped that she'd had enough of a lead to get to the apartment building first. Then maybe no one would get hurt. Maybe they'd have enough sense to stay outside and watch a cat climb a fire escape or chase the rats from their hiding places in the alleys.

Finally, with sore feet and sweat she knew was showing around her armpits, Becky reached the corner where everything had started. There was a bus stop with a fellow standing in the shadows, smoking a cigarette and waiting for the bus. Next to him was a fire hydrant and then a manhole cover flat against the ground. Becky wondered what things would be like if she could just will herself to be small enough to slip through the holes so she wouldn't have to go into that building. Now she regretted not grabbing a pack of cigarettes on the way.

Just as she was about to turn and ask the gent at the bus stop if she could bum a smoke, he had one arm around her waist and the other around her mouth.

"Don't make a move and I won't go for my gun," he said as he pulled her back into a thick border of bushes just off the sidewalk. Becky felt the spindly branches catch on her dress and stockings and scratch her skin as he backed up and out of view. The man held her close and tightly.

"Now, if I pull my hand away, will you be quiet?" he asked almost intimately in her ear. She nodded. Slowly he started to pull his hand away. "I think you knew my main squeeze, Violet."

Becky was frozen stiff. "You're Leonard Brennan. Her killer," she announced.

It only got Leonard to slap his hand over her mouth again, making her grunt.

"Is that what you think? I know who you are, girlie. You were the one working for Ferris. You snagged that flask, and now I want it back."

He jerked his arm around her waist, nearly crushing her ribs. Becky started to cough and gasp until Leonard finally let his hand off her mouth.

"I don't work for Ferris," Becky hissed. "What gave you that idea?"

"You were the one on the fire escape that day, weren't you?" he whispered close to her ear. "That hair is kind of hard to miss. And I knew you were friends with Violet. I thought you knew about them."

"I don't know what you're talking about," Becky huffed.

"You really don't work for Ferris?" Leonard asked, his grip loosening. "Because if you are lying to me, I don't have a problem teaching you a lesson."

"I'm sure of that. I saw what you did to Violet before you killed her. You bashed in her face. What's the matter, did she say hi to her doorman or maybe smile at a cab driver? She was one of the nicest girls I ever knew. You didn't deserve her."

"You might be right about that part. But I never laid a hand on Violet," Leonard said, his grip loose enough for Becky to whirl around and face him.

"How can you just stand there and lie? Have you no shame?" She scowled.

"It's true. Look, I have a reputation as a tough guy. I know that. But would you be surprised to know that I send my mama flowers every Mother's Day? And that my baby sister's birthday is December third, and I always take her to see Santa Claus at Gimbels Department Store?"

Becky couldn't see his face in the shadows. But she recognized his big shoulders and had seen his hands close up enough to know you couldn't impersonate mitts like those. This was Leonard Brennan.

"Every once in a while, I gotta set a fella straight. Sometimes he's amicable. Sometimes he needs a little persuading." He shrugged as if this was nothing more than a recipe for peach cobbler.

"So if you didn't kill Violet, who did?" Becky asked, but she was sure she knew the answer before Leonard said it.

"Officer Elby Ferris," Leonard said and clenched his fists.

"I was just on my way to see him. I do have the flask, but I'm making a trade," Becky said, stepping back so Leonard couldn't grab her again and take the only thing she had that would help get Fanny out.

"Please let me have it," Leonard pleaded.

"What good is it to you?" Becky asked.

"It's the only thing that ties Violet to Ferris. If he gets his hands on it, then I get the rap for killing her, because I was with her last. Everyone saw us together. Even you jumped to that conclusion." Becky heard Leonard swallow hard. "I loved her. I loved her, and she said she loved me but that it would never work. She had some hang-up about things she'd done in the past and the kind of family she had. None of it mattered to me. There was nothing she could have said or done that would have made me stop loving her."

Becky wasn't sure if this was some kind of flim-flam or if Leonard was telling the truth. She stood awkwardly in the bushes with him for a few seconds. When he finally spoke, he made her jump.

"I'll kill Ferris for what he did to her," he snarled.

"Why didn't you stop him before he killed Violet? I've seen the Brunos you associate with, and none of those guys look to be pushovers." Becky took a half step backward.

"I did it for her. She begged me not to interfere. She said as long as she did what Elby asked, me and my boys would be safe. She was some kind of woman." Leonard shook his head. "Look, you gotta get out of here. There's going to be a lot of Chicago lightning, and I wouldn't like it if you ended up in a pine box. So dust out. I mean scram," Leonard said, his soft demeanor instantly gone.

"Tell me one thing. Why were you chasing my friends and me at the club at 401 Portage?" Becky asked.

"I told you. I thought you were working for Ferris. Then when I saw you run into him when he was downstairs playing one of his games, I thought you were running to him for help," Leonard said.

"You were chatting, and that Miss Chantilly, she's like a bulldog most of the time. She don't let no one go traipsing around down there unless they pay the piper or got connections. I thought Ferris was your connection."

"What do you mean when you say Ferris was downstairs playing one of his games?" Becky didn't know why she asked. Perhaps she was getting more morbid as she got older. Maybe she wanted to believe that Elby Ferris wasn't as bad as he seemed.

She was instantly sorry she asked.

"Officer Elby Ferris is one of those guys who really enjoys hurting people. Especially women. The prettier they were, the worse he gave it to them. Violet got mixed up with him because he was conducting some kind of sting on one of her daddy's out-of-town friends," Leonard said. "He wasn't interested in some old geezer that liked to spend money on a young, pretty girl. Heck, every politician from dog catcher on up, I'll promise you, has a girl on the side."

"He set his sights on Violet, and there was nothing that was going to stop him from getting her. He roughed her up a lot. I'd go to her apartment and find her crying in a corner after he'd paid her a visit." Leonard shifted beneath his shirt, shrugging and stretching his neck to the left. "I should have killed him when I had the chance. I don't think Violet would have left me for that, do you?"

"I don't know, Leonard. All I do know is that Violet was a sweetheart. I don't reckon she'd treat you unfairly." It was all Becky could think to say.

"Look, like I said. There are going to be fireworks." Leonard looked at his watch. "You need to skedaddle. But please, give me the flask. Please."

"I wish I could, Leonard. Honest I do. But Elby Ferris kidnapped my cousin. He's got her in the basement of Violet's apartment. He's going to kill her if I don't give it to him. You have to understand I have to help her."

"He won't kill her. I promise you that. But he'll make her wish he would." Leonard took a deep breath. "Okay. This is what we do."

He stooped down at least a foot to speak quietly and give Becky not just directions on what to do but also a little hope that she and Fanny might come out of this yet.

## CHAPTER TWENTY-FOUR

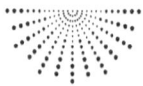

*B*ecky walked across the street from the bus stop to the building she knew had been Violet's residence. Skirting around the corner, she walked toward the alley. A man as wide as he was short stepped out of the shadows with a gun pointed at her.

"We've been expecting you, doll. Right this way." He jerked the gun to the right.

Becky had instantly put her hands up at the sight of the man and kept them there as she walked down the alley toward another man, whose neck stretched about an additional five inches above his collar, showcasing an Adam's apple that made it look as if he had swallowed a golf ball.

Becky eyeballed the lanky guy, and as soon as

she got to the door, she stopped. Her heart was pounding, but she tried to remain calm. This was going to be no different than exchanging a pair of shoes at the department store. A creepy, dirty department store. She tapped her foot and folded her arms.

"Okay, sweetheart. The boss is expecting you," Mr. Adam's apple said. His voice was like a low note on a saxophone.

"What? I have to get the door myself?" Becky huffed.

"Oh, pardon me, Duchess. Did you hear her, Kenny? She doesn't want to get the door for herself." Mr. Adam's Apple was really in a dither over Becky's antics.

"Oh, well allow me," Short and Stout replied as he barged past Becky, nearly knocking her over as he got to the door and yanked it open. "Now get inside before I kick you inside."

This was obviously the service entrance. The janitor of the building probably used it, as did the garbage men. It smelled like pipes and dripping water. The floor was an ugly concrete, and the walls were painted a deep green that she was sure hid a world of sins. There had to be dozens of stains, spills, and streaks of every kind dripping down. It was nothing like Lucretia's fine, spotless yellow kitchen.

Why that particular memory of home popped into Becky's head she couldn't be sure, but she hated that it did. The chance she might never see it again made her chest tighten and her eyes start to water. Without thinking, Becky bit down on her tongue as hard as she could stand and felt the tears recede.

There was nothing but one pale, naked bulb hanging precariously from a rather jagged wire in the middle of the hallway to give her any guidance. At the end of the hallway was an open door. She could hear softly murmuring voices as well as shuffling footsteps. The one thing Becky didn't hear was Fanny.

It was as if the hallway kept stretching out in front of her, and it was going to take her hours to get to the end. She swallowed and took a deep breath to keep her head. She just needed to get to Fanny. Then she'd let the plan unfold. If she could just get to Fanny and make sure she was all right, then nothing else mattered.

Her footsteps echoed, making her look behind her to see if Mr. Adam's Apple or Mr. Short and Stout was sneaking up. But there was no one there. Just the shadows swallowing the end of the hall stared back at her. When she turned around to face forward, she noticed thick spider webs in the corner of the ceiling and shivered.

Finally, at the door at the end of the hall, she peeked inside and saw Fanny.

"Fanny!" Becky was about to run to her, but a huge mountain of a man stepped in her way, making her stop short and nearly lose her balance. Fanny was sitting in a chair, her arms folded properly in her lap. She had a smudge of dirt on her cheek, and her clothes looked a little dirty, but other than that, she was in one piece.

"Becky! This is all your fault. I just know it!" Fanny shouted. "You're always into things that you're not supposed to be. Why can't you ever learn to mind your own business?"

"Oh, that's rich coming from you. You never met a conversation in my house that you didn't stop and listen to, whether it was your business or not," Becky replied, her blood instantly boiling. "Mind my business? That's all you ever do is mind *my* business!"

"You go on ahead and throw insults. But this blouse cost me a dollar and fifteen cents," Fanny spat. "I'll expect to be repaid."

"Oh, because saving your derriere isn't good enough. I wouldn't have to do this if you had a lick of sense and knew how to handle yourself. You could have started talking about Paris and bored these guys to death if nothing else!"

Becky began to stomp up to Fanny, but the big palooka in her way refused to let her pass. "What is wrong with you? Let me pass!" Becky shouted at him.

"Don't let her anywhere near me! She's got a screw loose!" Fanny hollered. "I am telling your mother, Rebecca Madeline!"

"You think you'll be able to talk after I knock your tee—" Becky was ready to charge her cousin, but the tension in the room quickly escalated and froze her feet in place.

"Would you two shut up!" Elby Ferris emerged from the corner of the room.

Becky hadn't even seen him, and if Fanny knew he was there, she hadn't paid any attention to him until now. He was wearing his police uniform, but the jacket was unbuttoned, revealing a white undershirt. His chest was broad, and it was obvious he was in good shape, as the undershirt clung to his pectorals and flat stomach. A guy didn't get to this level in a life of crime by being soft all over. But the glassy redness had returned to his eyes. His forehead glistened as he started to sweat. It wasn't hot in the room. As Becky's blood pressure dropped back to normal, she felt a severe chill in the air. But still, Elby Ferris looked like he was running a fever. Maybe he was.

"Give me what you stole," he snapped at Becky.

"Let Fanny go, and I'll tell you where it is," Becky said, looking up at the big man in front of her.

"Do you really think you are in any position to dictate how this is going to happen?" Elby sneered.

Becky watched him slowly walk up to Fanny. Her cousin was oblivious to the real danger she was in. Fanny had convinced herself the worst that could happen already had: that she was going to have a ruined outfit. But at the end, she'd be able to walk out of here, snitch to Aunt Kitty, and go back to her stories about Paris.

"I'm telling you now that if you do anything to my cousin, I won't tell you where I put the flask. It's not far from here. This big palooka can step outside and pick it up in two minutes." Becky's voice trembled. Her whole body was a sheet of sweat and her heart was racing. She had thought this was going to be easier than this. Why had she thought that? She had put her trust in a guy who she knew was a kneecap breaker at best. What had she been thinking?

"Oh, I think you are going to tell me where it is. And then, once I have it, you and your pretty cousin and I are going to have a nice long talk and get to know one another. Become real pals," Elby said.

Before Becky could say anything else, he raised his hand and struck Fanny hard across the face. The poor girl was stunned. Her eyes instantly welled with tears, and she looked to Becky.

"You monster! Don't you touch her!" Becky leapt forward, but the big goon had her around the waist with one arm, laughing as she kicked and scratched and tried to bite.

"Tell me what I want to know," Elby said in a horrible, singsongy kind of way. He was taunting her.

Had Becky been able to break free, she would have scratched his eyes out. But the more she struggled, the tighter this goon squeezed, until she was practically choking.

"Just let her go!" Becky pleaded. "I'll stay in her place. You haven't lost anything. I'll tell you where it is, but please, just let my cousin go. She's so dippy, she will have forgotten everything by tomorrow. Please, let her go."

"You know, I really like hearing a woman with manners. I'm glad you know how to say please.

You're going to be saying it a lot," Elby hissed. He grabbed Fanny's hand and started to bend her pinky finger backward.

"No!" Becky shouted.

Fanny began to cry and beg for Elby not to break her finger.

"She's got nine more. And I bet she's got pretty painted red toenails too." He gritted his teeth as he smiled and pulled her finger farther apart from the digits it was meant to stay close to. Fanny's face was a twisted mess of dripping mascara and pain.

"It's under a bucket just outside the alley! It's just outside the alley! It's there. Please stop!" Becky screamed.

Elby still had Fanny's hand. For a minute, Becky was afraid he was going to do it anyway. Like pulling a drumstick off a turkey, he would break her pinky just because he could. But he let her go. Fanny pulled her hand to her chest, cradling it.

Elby ordered the guy who was holding Becky back to go get it. He turned her loose, only for Becky to lose her footing and fall to the ground with a thud.

"You'll see that I am a very reasonable man. I don't ask for much," Elby said as he stroked Fanny's hair. She leaned away from his touch.

"Leave her alone. Fanny! Just go. Get up and go!" Becky shouted as she got to her feet. But Fanny was like a deer in the headlights. She looked up at Elby, who was looming over her. His intentions were oozing from his pores, but still Fanny didn't fight. She couldn't. She didn't have it in her. Instead, Fanny fainted.

"Oh, for Pete's sake." Becky rolled her eyes then narrowed them on Elby. "You can leave her alone now. You're getting what you want. Or are you? I hope you trusted that buffoon you sent out there. He wouldn't turn on you, would he? It sure is taking him a long time to get back."

The look on Elby's face after Becky uttered those words made her wish she'd kept her mouth shut.

# CHAPTER TWENTY-FIVE

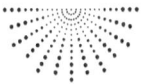

*O*fficer Elby Ferris yanked off his police uniform jacket, dropped it on the dusty concrete floor, and stomped up to Becky. When she stepped back and put her arms up to defend herself she again lost her balance and nearly fell to the ground. It was only Elby's viselike grip around her wrist, yanking her to her feet, that stopped her.

"You've got a smart mouth," he spat. "That's the problem with you women. You think that you can do and say whatever you want. Well, you are going to learn your place. But only after I teach that pretty cousin of yours a thing or two."

"You aren't going to lay a hand on her," Becky said through clenched teeth.

The bones in her wrist were on fire as Elby

squeezed it. She was sure with a little more pressure, he was going to break it. Her eyes began to water as much from anger as from pain. What kind of man did this to a woman? Didn't any of his fellow officers know about him? Wasn't there anyone who could put a stop to him?

Stretching her mouth open in a silent scream, Becky was about to start begging for mercy. She hated herself for it. She hated that he'd bested her. But she was slowly sinking to her knees, her armpits drenched with sweat, her body shaking as she tried to pull his fingers off. But it was impossible. He had her, and she was not going to get away. Not this time. Becky thought it funny that she was now going to be one of the dead people she was so used to seeing in the most unusual places.

Becky held her breath. She looked past Elby to Fanny. What was she doing? Did she think she could somehow stop him? But when she saw Fanny, she gasped. Her eyes widened, and she desperately scratched and pulled at Elby's hand to get away from not just him but the thing behind him.

The small bulb hanging from the ceiling in this room and the single bulb out in the hallway began to flicker. Elby stopped. He looked at Becky as if she was causing it. Suddenly, the temperature in the room became freezing cold. Becky could see her breath as she panted. Elby's grip had loosened enough that she was no longer in pain. But he wasn't letting her go.

In between the flickers of light, a black mass began to form. It spun and writhed and slinked around the space, coming up from the floor like steam from a heater. Becky's heart began to race.

"Got it, boss." The big man finally returned. He was out of breath, as if he had done two dozen chin-ups along the way, and his face was red.

"What's wrong with the lights?" Elby growled.

"How should I know? I ain't no electrician. These parts of the buildings ain't never wired right. Probably just a short," he said as he stepped forward, his extended hand holding the silver flask.

"That's not it," Becky mumbled.

"Shut up, you. Want me to take her, boss? I know just what to do with—"

The fat man froze as soon as he saw it. The black thing was moving faster, as if it was getting angrier. It swirled and jabbed and folded over and around itself before it began to slide across the floor. It was moving toward Fanny.

"No!" Becky screamed. "Stay away from her!"

"What are you yelling about?" Elby hadn't

noticed. His lust for pain and suffering had distracted him from the thing that was creeping along behind him.

"Boss? What is that?" The fat man pointed.

Finally, Elby turned around and saw it. The glassy, fevered look in his eyes suddenly disappeared. It was as if he instantly sobered up. His mouth fell open, and he stared at the thing as it travelled across the floor toward Fanny.

"Stay away from her!" Becky screamed again.

But it was too late. The black thing descended on her quickly, making Fanny's body shake and twitch. Tears streamed down Becky's cheeks as she watched helplessly. It was going to kill her. It was going to kill them all.

"Elby?" Fanny spoke, but it wasn't her voice.

Finally, Elby let go of Becky's wrist. He stared at Fanny.

"What is this? Is this some kind of joke? A trick?" he stuttered. Becky shook her head. "What are you and your cousin up to? What do you think you're doing impersonating her? I ought to kill you right now."

"Don't you touch her," Fanny said. But it wasn't Fanny. It was Violet, and she was inside Fanny, like when she had been sleepwalking and ended up at Becky's vanity.

"This isn't happening!" Elby shouted. "You two witches are playing a trick!"

"Elby, do you remember all those things you said to me?" Violet asked as she lifted Fanny's head, and her eyes popped open. They were piercing black stones, hard and hypnotizing.

The fat man let out a yelp like a wounded puppy. For the first time in probably years, he didn't ask his boss for permission to move. He turned and ran for the door. There was a loud noise as if he'd crashed through the wall to get away from what he was witnessing.

"Violet? Is that really you?" Elby asked.

"You know it's me. Don't you know your lover when you hear her voice?" Fanny's face and blond hair slowly began to melt into those of the raven-haired beauty.

"This isn't happening. You're doing this." He scowled at Becky, unaware his henchman had just left him holding the bag. With one quick snap of his wrist, he grabbed Becky's collar and yanked her to within inches of his face. "You put a spell on me." Spit flew in her face. "I'll teach you a lesson you won't soon forget. I hope you told your mama you love her, because you're never gonna see her again."

"I didn't," Becky said, squaring her shoulders as best she could. "I think this is just your past catching up with you."

"I still feel so sorry for you, Elby. You were never very smart. But then again, I guess I wasn't either," Violet cooed.

Elby was sure Becky was the one doing the talking. But how could she be? He was looking right at her when he heard that voice. He had been watching Becky's face. She didn't speak. So who did? He whirled around. His Adam's apple bounced when he swallowed.

Becky wondered if the part of the plan Leonard Brennan had proposed was happening now. By this time, Mr. Adam's Apple and Short and Stout should be as helpless as kittens, and Leonard should be busting his way in. But so far, everything was quiet.

"Do you remember what you used to say to me?" Violet asked, taking a step in Elby's direction. "You used to tell me I was nothing without you. That you knew where I came from and that I'd never be anything more than white trash."

"That was just the booze talking," Elby replied. "You know how I felt about you. But sometimes you made me so mad. You wouldn't stop, and I'd lose my temper. But I never meant to hurt you, baby. I never did."

Becky didn't dare move. Nor did she blink or breathe. Her gaze went to Elby as Violet continued speaking.

"I know you haven't forgotten." She slinked another step closer but stopped. "You were going to get Leonard any way you could. But the problem was, he was too smart for the likes of you. He had you against the ropes, didn't he?"

"He did not!" Elby barked. "He was a two-bit hood. I'm a policeman on the Savannah Police Department! I call the shots in these parts!"

"He loved me, plain and simple. He didn't care where I came from. We were both broken, but together, we were whole. You hated that, didn't you, Elby?" Violet's voice echoed. Every word reverberated in Elby's head like blow after blow.

"I told you, you were *mine*. I gave you all those pretty things. Furs! Diamonds! You never turned me down. You weren't innocent in all this. Do you hear me? You weren't innocent!" Elby was losing control. "I had to keep you away from him, but you wouldn't do as you were told! You wouldn't listen!"

"Tell me, Elby. Do you have a new girl yet? Have

you found someone who fell for your lies and tolerated your bullying? Tell me, Elby. How many girls ended up like me?" Violet hissed.

"I don't have no one, baby. It was always you," Elby lied.

"That's not true!" Becky screamed. "He's lying to you again."

Elby flung his arm back, hitting Becky in the side of the head and knocking her to the ground. She sat up, shook her noggin, and put her hand to her head.

"I don't think you'll be romancing anyone anymore, Elby. Do me a favor? Tell me again what you said before you killed me. Just say it once more." Violet's voice was soft and forgiving, even if her words weren't.

"I said... that I loved you." Elby winced as if the words were painful coming out of his mouth.

"You did, didn't you," Violet said. "And then you did this." She turned around.

Becky gasped. The back of her head was missing. It wasn't as simple as the papers had said. It was a mangled mess, and no matter how hard Becky tried to tell herself it wasn't really Fanny, she couldn't help feeling her heart being torn to shreds.

"Violet. I didn't know." Elby took a step toward her.

"No," Becky whispered. Violet was using Fanny's body. If Elby tried to do anything, he'd be hurting Fanny, not Violet. Violet was already dead. Becky tried to move, but her legs weren't responding. It was almost as if they'd become glued in place.

"Elby, my darling." Violet turned back around to face her murderer. "You have a sickness in your head. I can help you now like I couldn't before. Come to me, Elby."

He took another step. Becky saw him reach into his pocket. He pulled something out and held it at his side.

"No," Becky hissed again.

Her voice was gone. Her movements were heavy and slow, as if she'd been shackled by invisible weights. Something was holding her back. Suddenly she began to panic. Her heart started racing as Elby inched closer. As she stared, trying to focus, she finally saw what he was holding in his hand. It was a gun. He was going to kill Fanny in an attempt to kill the ghost of the woman he murdered. It was a confusing mess like a string of jewelry that was knotted and tangled. But the main point was he was going to kill Fanny.

"Violet, you were my girl. I didn't want to share

you with anyone. I was jealous, baby. I made a mistake," Elby soothed as he approached.

That was when the gun went off.

Becky jumped. She stared at Fanny, expecting her body to fold up and sink to the ground. But she didn't. She remained on her feet. Officer Elby Ferris whirled around, aimed his gun at the door with a shaking, dying hand, and squeezed off a round before falling to the ground.

# CHAPTER TWENTY-SIX

*B*efore Becky could make a move, she saw Leonard Brennan walk in. He was holding his gun, and a deep red splotch on the front of his shirt was spreading.

"Baby, is that really you?" he asked. His voice was deep and kind.

"Lenny. I should have run off with you when I had the chance. I'm so sorry," Violet said.

"You don't ever have to be sorry with me, Vi," he said as he shuffled up to Fanny, who was still Violet. "I love you."

Leonard took Fanny in his arms and kissed her. It was the kind of kiss that could have ignited even the coldest heart. Their kiss reminded Becky of the way Adam had kissed her the other night when they had been hiding beneath the stairs. For those brief seconds, Violet was still alive as Leonard took his last breath, filled with her perfume, feeling the softness of her skin and the feathery tickle of her jet-black hair against his cheek.

With his dying gaze, Leonard saw Violet perfect and whole. He smiled at her with tears in his eyes as he fell to the floor, dead. At that same moment, Violet's image faded away, leaving Fanny standing there with her blouse and skirt stained with blood and two dead men at her feet. But before she disappeared, she said one last thing.

"You're a swell egg, Becky."

Becky's heart lodged in her throat. If only she could have thought of something to say back to Violet. If only she was quicker on her feet. But she stood there like a dummy and watched as Fanny came back in to focus.

"Oh my lands! What is going on? Becky!" Fanny screamed.

Becky jumped up and ran to her cousin to take her in her arms and hug her tightly. But Fanny slapped her hands away.

"What did you do? You killed these two men!"

"What?" Becky shouted.

"You slipped me a mickey or something, and you killed these two men. There's no one else here! Who else could have done it? I didn't do it. And I'm not covering for you. This is too much," Fanny whined.

"I didn't kill anybody. These two palookas killed each other. At least I think they did."

Becky ran over to Elby. He was on his back, his eyes staring blankly into the great abyss. Becky felt around on his body and decided he was dead as a doornail. She did the same to Leonard. The only difference between the two men was that Elby looked as if one of his legs was caught in a bear trap. Leonard looked like he was asleep.

"Now come on. We have to get out of here!" Becky grabbed Fanny by the wrist and gave her a yank.

"I swear I've never been through such trauma. I'm not sure I can make it." Fanny let Becky half drag her out of the basement.

Outside the door in a heap was the fat man who had left in a hurry. He had a lump on his head, but he was still breathing.

"What do we do about him?" Fanny asked.

"What are you talking about? We leave him here," Becky replied before patting him down, rifling through his pockets for something and slipping it down her blouse.

"Are you robbing him? Rebecca Mackenzie, you are beyond help. What if he's hurt?"

"He *is* hurt. He has a goose egg on that dome from someone putting his lights out. Do you want to stay here and wait until he wakes up? Ask him if he needs a doctor or maybe a stiff drink? Because I'll leave you here if that's what you want to do," Becky huffed.

Fanny said nothing and let her cousin pull her down the hallway to the exit.

Becky pushed the door open, and there, lying on the ground, were Mr. Adam's Apple and Short and Stout. They, too, were unconscious. Before Fanny could open her mouth to voice another complaint, the sound of an approaching mob froze them both.

"I think it's around here. Is it around here? Are we on the right block?" a familiar voice babbled on.

"I can't believe you let her give us the slip." This voice Becky recognized as Teddy's.

"She was so smooth about it. Oh, if she gets herself killed, I'll never forgive her," Martha barked. "Where could she be?"

"Oh, Teddy!" Fanny shouted.

"Wait, I hear something." The other familiar voice was Stephen.

From around the corner of the alley, Stephen, Martha, and Teddy appeared. Martha nearly fainted when she saw Fanny covered in blood.

"Thank goodness it's y'all," Fanny huffed.

"Take this girl and get her out of here quick," Becky said as if she was doing nothing more than getting ready to go home from a speakeasy.

"Becky, that was a foolish thing you did, giving us the run-around like you did. What happened?" Stephen demanded.

Becky looked up at him and was about to speak, but Fanny interrupted.

"Becky killed two men and left three others lying unconscious on the ground. She robbed one of them," she huffed.

It was as if the entire city fell silent, and only the sound of crickets could be heard.

"It didn't quite happen like that. Look, I'll fill in the blanks as soon as we get out of here," Becky said.

"Are you all right? You look hurt," Stephen said, looking at the side of Becky's face. She'd forgotten that Officer Ferris had given her a lick, and only now did she feel the sting and swelling around her eye.

"Oh, just a love tap from Mr. Wonderful in there. But he got his," Becky said, grabbing Stephen by the sleeve and pulling him toward the alley.

Fanny was desperately clinging to Teddy, her left arm linked through his right arm, while pulling on Martha's sleeve. Her mouth hadn't stopped running since Violet left her body. She was babbling and gasping and loving every minute of the undivided attention.

"You were lucky Becky came for you," Martha said.

"Lucky? Why, it's her fault I ended up here. Kidnapped. This sort of thing was never even a consideration when I was staying with Grammy Louise in Paris. The thought never crossed my mind that I might be kidnapped. I guess some members of the family are just higher brow than others," Fanny huffed. Off in the distance, sirens grew louder.

"Do you think they're headed this way?" Teddy looked at Martha.

"I don't want to risk it. We better cheese it outta here."

They started to run through the alley in the direction of Teddy's car. Stephen grabbed Becky by the hand, and they followed. Just as everyone piled into Teddy's flivver, two police cars zoomed by, and it looked as if they were heading to the building in which Violet had died a short while ago.

On the way home, Fanny sat in the front seat between Teddy and Martha. She ran her gums the entire time, explaining how she had no idea what had happened. That one second, Stephen had been standing next to her, and the next he was gone and she was alone, being pushed into that dingy basement by a goon with the muzzle of a gun in her back.

"No thanks to Becky," she huffed.

"Are you crazy?" Martha interrupted. "Becky was desperate to get to you. She was in a dither and beside herself when she found out you'd been taken by those animals. You never saw a woman so agitated."

"Well, if she didn't associate with the wrong kind of people, none of this would have happened." There was no convincing Fanny that Becky had done anything other than get her scared out of her wits and her blouse and skirt ruined.

With Stephen sitting on her right-hand side in the back seat, Becky looked off to the left. And she realized that the nicest words her Cousin Fanny had ever said to her had come when Fanny had been possessed by a girl with a questionable reputation.

She took a deep breath and let it out slowly. In that moment, Stephen slipped his hand around hers and squeezed it. She looked at him, his face still redder and bumpier than usual, and smiled sadly. He smiled back, not letting go of her hand until they were back at the Mackenzie plantation.

# CHAPTER TWENTY-SEVEN

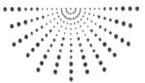

*B*ecky heard the commotion downstairs and looked at the clock on her bedroom nightstand. It was barely five in the morning, and she heard her mother calling from the front door. Without even trying to slip on her slippers or her robe, Becky dashed out of her room and down the hallway. Bounding two steps at a time, she ran to her mother's arms.

"Oh, my dear, sweet girl! I missed you so much!" Kitty cried. Anyone would have thought she'd spent time at the front lines of the War of Northern Aggression the way she was hugging and kissing Becky. "Oh my, I think you've grown since I left. Oh, I've got a surprise for you. Actually, I have more than one."

Judge could be heard stomping down the hallway from the other end of the house.

"What in the world is all this ruckus?" he teased. "Oh, it's just my two favorite gals." He walked over to Kitty with his arms wide. She left Becky to hug her husband tightly and bury her face in his chest.

"Judge, please don't make me go visit my relatives without you again," Kitty sighed.

"Did everything work out, Mama? Did Aunt Hortense pass peacefully?" Becky asked, trying not to come across rudely.

"Aunt Hortense? I do believe that she plans on outliving Methuselah," Kitty replied with pursed lips. "Her son Carl's fiancée, Linnie, had words with the woman, and the wedding is off."

"It's off?" Judge gasped, making Becky snicker.

"Yes, and wouldn't you know that as soon as Linnie announced she was moving back to Cotton-wood, Aunt Hortense got up out of bed and began to cook breakfast for everyone," Kitty said as if it were the work of divine intervention.

"Then Aunt Mimi caught Aunt Tilly admiring some of the fine silver your Aunt Hortense has collected over the years, and a huge brawl broke out there. Aunt Tilly told Aunt Mimi that she didn't get more just because she can breed like a rabbit. Then

Mimi replied that there was no inheritance for cheaters and went so far as to point at Tilly's husband." Kitty was nearly out of breath when she finished. "I swear, I thought there was going to be a cat fight for sure. And here you are going to speakeasies and parties when you can get all the excitement you want just by visiting family. Why, I didn't even tell you about Aunt Hortense taking a carving knife after Linnie before Linnie decided to call off the wedding."

"Pulled a carving knife?" Judge's eyes bugged.

"Oh yes. I've only given you the highlight reel. The feature presentation was even grander. And I don't think I've ever gone so long without a full night of sleep in my life." Kitty flopped down on her favorite chair in the parlor as Judge picked up her bags.

"I, for one, want to hear all about it," he said on his way to the bedroom to drop the luggage, stopping only to kiss Kitty on the head in passing.

"Me too."

"Oh, Rebecca. What a relief to be home. I did meet a very nice gentleman while I was there who said he may be paying a visit to Savannah sometime soon and would love to stop a spell for a visit." Kitty batted her eyes.

"Mama, why must you torture me?" Becky asked.

"We won't talk about it now. How did you and your cousin get along while I was gone?" Kitty asked. "I know it was an awful burden having to tend to her all by yourself. I know your father couldn't have been much help with two young women to keep occupied."

"Well, she's still alive, so I guess I managed," Becky said. "Of course, I'm not sure what she'll have to say about me. You know, they do so many things so differently in Paris. Oh, Mama, before she gets up, I have to tell you about Martha. She had one too many and insisted that Fanny didn't go to Paris, France, but was actually in Paris, Texas. Fanny was fit to be tied."

"Oh, I'm going to have to have a talk with that Martha." Kitty furrowed her brows before chuckling. "And when do you think I should talk with your father?"

"About what?" Becky asked innocently.

"About his poker game." Kitty smirked.

"I don't know what you're talking about," Becky said. "If Daddy had a poker game, it was the quietest, most civil poker game in history, because I know nothing about it, and I was home almost every night."

"Now I know you're lying. Shame on you, Becky," Kitty said. She grabbed her daughter's hands, pulling her in for a bear hug.

Becky knelt in front of her mother and squeezed her back. She smelled of lavender, and her mother's cotton dress was crisp and soft against her cheek. "Oh, and even though you are lying to your one and only mother, I have a gift for you. Bring me my satchel over there by the front door."

Becky got up, still in her bare feet, padded over, and grabbed the bag. It was heavy, and she needed to use both hands.

"Did you bring Aunt Hortense back with you?" she joked.

"I wouldn't bring that woman a glass of water," Kitty mumbled, making Becky gasp. Kitty Mackenzie was the epitome of Southern style and grace, and speaking ill of someone, especially kin, was strictly low class. Unless the person in question was of the most unsavory reputation or had worn out their welcome, which Aunt Hortense obviously had.

Kitty unzipped the bag and pulled out a package wrapped in brown paper with a red string around it.

"On one of my trips to town, I saw this in a window and wondered who in the world would want such a thing. Then I remembered, oh yes, my one and only daughter would." Kitty smiled.

Becky plopped down on the floor as if it was Christmas morning and unwrapped a leather-bound sketchbook with gold on the edges of the pages and a red ribbon bookmark.

"Mama, it's beautiful," she said, her eyes filling with tears.

"Now maybe you can draw some pictures of all your friends and your family and have a nice history to pass on to your children someday," Kitty said, smoothing Becky's wild hair.

"I will. I'll do just that," Becky promised just before Judge came back into the room. She jumped up and ran to her father to show him her lovely gift.

Just then, a groggy Fanny came shuffling into the room.

"Oh, you're back. Welcome home, Aunt Kitty," Fanny said. "We missed you terribly. But as you can see, the house is still standing. Uncle Judge's poker party did attract the police, but no harm was done."

Judge cleared his throat as Becky held her new sketchbook up to her nose, hiding her smirk as she inhaled the delicious smell of real leather. Kitty looked at Judge with the same smirk and stood from her seat.

"Well, that is good to know. So, the police arrived? And you knew nothing about it? Well, I'm glad no real harm was done."

Becky couldn't help but laugh and elbow her daddy. Kitty gave Fanny a quick peck on the cheek before walking over to her husband. On tiptoe, she kissed his cheek as well.

"Anyone for coffee?" Kitty asked, to which everyone said yes.

$\sim$

several days had gone by since Becky and Fanny had narrowly escaped from the sadistic clutches of Officer Elby Ferris. He had been given a hero's funeral and was being hailed as a dedicated officer who had stood against organized crime and paid for it with his life.

Meanwhile, Leonard Brennan was eulogized as a thug with a criminal record who was suspected of several unsolved crimes, including the murder of Violet Darcy.

Fanny squawked enough about the buck fifteen that her skirt and blouse had cost that Becky gave her four dollars to go away somewhere and get a new dress. She found herself some scandalous red thing that made even a blind man pushing pencils on the street do a double take.

"That girl doesn't hide much, does she," Martha said as they walked to 401 Portage.

Since the troubling element that had frightened Becky the first time they'd visited the joint was now gone and there were no reports of any witnesses seeing a redhead or a blond at the scene of the double murder, Becky thought they could give the place another chance. She shrugged and rolled her eyes at Martha's comment.

"So, your mama is home now? Did she have a good time in Alabama?" Martha changed the subject.

"Who can have a good time in Alabama? Besides, she was with the kin whose branch on the family tree has few offshoots." Becky chuckled. "Minus the murders, she had as much commotion out there as we had over here."

As they slipped into the speakeasy, Becky instantly began to feel better. Since the incident in the basement, she'd had the feeling something had changed. Fanny was exactly the same. She had not ratted Becky out as she'd threatened to do, probably because it might jeopardize her own status in the Mackenzie house and force her to relocate to another home where she might not be so well received.

Fanny had no recollection of anything Becky had said or done during the whole kidnapping and rescue. If she did, she refused to talk about it. Even if Becky took the time to explain how worried she had been and how she would have done anything to get her out of there, Fanny would never see past her own nose. It was just how she was. Fanny remembered how she felt and how she looked and what she was thinking—if anyone believed the girl ever had a thought form in her head. Thankfully, she knew enough to keep her trap shut and not discuss the incident with outsiders. For as empty as her head was, a tiny sliver of common sense had managed to lodge itself somewhere between her ears.

"What can I get you ladies?" Teddy asked. He also hadn't changed and was as charming as ever. Tonight he had donned his straw hat with a blue band and his brown two-toned shoes.

"Champagne cocktail." Becky snapped her fingers.

"Ditto," said Martha.

Fanny had already had her drink ordered by a dapper-looking alderman with a gold pocket watch and a pencil mustache.

Martha continued to chew Becky's ear, and Becky was thankful for it. That was what made her a really good friend. Martha knew Becky so well that she understood when Becky needed to be quiet but that she didn't want to be alone.

"I know you don't want to talk about it, but that whole incident did something to you," Martha said in Becky's ear over the snare drum and trumpet that were busting up the joint.

Becky looked at her, but no words would come. She couldn't tell her to go fly a kite, because Martha was one hundred percent right. But she couldn't put her finger on what it was that had changed, so she wasn't able to agree with her. Instead, she shrugged again, rolling her eyes.

"You can't fool me." Martha took her drink in her hand and raised it to Becky before taking a sip. "Something happened with Fanny that changed you. What did she do?"

Becky's chest seized up, and she held her breath. How could Martha have figured that out? Before Becky could shake away the comment as if it were hogwash, the words just began to tumble out of her mouth.

"She slapped my hands away. After those two jamokes had offed each other, she yelled for me. I was so relieved she was all right. I jumped up and ran to give her a hug, and she slapped my hands away." Becky took a deep gulp from her champagne cocktail. "The worst part is that I don't know why I care. I don't even like her."

"That's easy. She's kin. And who can you rely on if it ain't your kin?" Martha continued talking as she looked through her clutch. "Just take a step back and look at it from her point of view. She's the one with all the looks—sorry, but she is."

Becky couldn't disagree. Fanny was rife with the qualities so desired by the opposite sex.

"She's travelled to Europe. Everyone who has talked to her for five minutes knows this."

Becky grinned and nodded.

"Then, what else is there?" Martha raised her eyebrows as she looked up from her clutch. "Then there is you. You ain't hurtin' in the looks department. And in addition to that cuteness, you got a personality that attracts people like bees to honey. You can *and will* dance with anyone regardless of their state in life. Face it, Rebecca. You are a good gal. And she's jealous."

"You sound like Judge," Becky said, blushing at the compliment.

"Your daddy is right. Now, do you have a ciggy? I

have been dying for one, and I think I left my case at home," Martha said just as Teddy approached.

"They're playing our song, toots. What do you say?" He put his hand out, and Martha immediately clamped on.

"I'll be right back," she said to Becky.

"I'll make sure I stay lit," Becky joked.

She reached into her clutch and realized she'd grabbed Violet's flask. When she touched it tenderly, she saw the initials and said a quick prayer for Violet.

Popping a cigarette into her mouth, she looked up at the people on the dance floor. Once again, they were crammed like sardines except for a cute couple off to the right in the corner. She had beautiful black hair and loads of ice on each wrist. He was a tall, muscular fellow with a serious look on his face. They held each other close as they danced to the slow, romantic song the band was playing. No one was paying any attention to them. It was as if Becky was the only one who could see them as they swayed together. He said something into her ear, and she leaned back, smiling, happy. They kissed.

Becky looked down at the bar to scoop up a book of matches. When she looked back, the couple was gone. In their place was a tall, handsome guy who was staring at her. He was wearing a cap, and the sleeves of his work shirt were rolled up to his elbows. It was Adam. He waved and made his way over to her.

Her heart began to race, and she started to feel like herself again.

# ABOUT THE AUTHOR

Harper Lin is a *USA TODAY* bestselling cozy mystery author.

When she's not reading or writing, she loves hiking, doing yoga, and hanging out with her family and friends.

For a complete list of her books by series, visit her website.

www.HarperLin.com